The ~~...........~~

Taking a train full of currency or capturing a Spanish treasure ship is nothing compared to the greatest theft in history—when the captain of a company of English archers and his men stole the entire treasury and religious relics of the world's greatest and richest empire and escaped to Cornwall with chests and chests of gold coins and priceless relics. This is part of the story of how it happened.

Preface

This is another of the books in an exciting and action-packed saga about an English serf who rose to become the captain of a company of English archers and fought his way to riches beyond his wildest dreams—and forever changed medieval and modern England. The other books in this exciting medieval saga about an English serf's rise to wealth and power are also available on Kindle. They can be found as eBooks on Amazon. Search for *Martin Archer books.*

The parchments on which this novel is based were found some years ago in a trunk buried under a pile of rubble in the Bodelian Library basement. What follows in this exciting novel was mostly taken from the parchments written by William, a serf from Kent, describing his experiences and battles as he rose in the years after King Richard's crusade to become the captain of a company of English archers and a rich man. Other sources were parchments describing the activities and thoughts of his priestly brother Thomas, his son George, and several of his key lieutenants and sergeants.

A *Company of Archers* book
The Missing Treasure

Chapter One
The unexpected state of things.

"What do you mean all the gold and coins are missing?"

"It's true, I tell you. I was just there. They're gone. The room is empty—the chests are gone."

He hadn't been running but he was literally out of breath from the shock of seeing what he had seen in the windowless room next to the emperor's sleeping chamber—nothing, absolutely nothing. It was empty.

"My God. Are you sure? What will Alexios do now?"

"I don't care about him. What will happen to us when we tell him? We're the ones in danger and there's no half way about it."

The two men are cousins and both of them are supporters of the son of one of the empire's previous emperors, the man had been blinded and replaced by his brother who had taken his place as emperor and had recently fled in the night on a galley provided by the English archers. It was the son who had promised the crusaders much of the gold in the Byzantine Empire's treasury if they would help him get his blind father back on the throne.

The two Greeks were beside themselves with worry and rightly so. The emperor disappeared from his empire's great capitol city of Constantinople weeks ago, right after the crusaders came to the city's walls from their camp across the inlet and began their attack. He'd somehow escaped from the city with all the gold and jewels in the treasury.

Everyone in the city knew within hours that the emperor had run and many of the empire's leaders had either gone with him or they'd run themselves when they found out he was gone; what they and the blind man's young son and new co-emperor wouldn't know for a few more minutes is that the fleeing emperor had totally emptied the treasury before he left. He'd taken the empire's entire treasury of coins, gold, and jewels with him into exile.

We English know what happened to the emperor and his courtiers, of course we do; it was our galleys that were paid handsomely to carry them to safety. And we know something else; the emperor and his courtiers only think they got away with the gold and coins and such from the treasury and have personally hidden it away where only they know where to find it. In fact, the emperor and his men only think they have the gold and coins safely hidden; they don't—we took them to Cornwall.

******

Initially the crusaders had merely been camping across

the waterway from Constantinople's walls and demanding that the old emperor be restored to the throne. They knew he was blind and old and they thought he was rich because the emperor, and only the emperor, controls the treasury of the great and rich and far flung Byzantine Empire.

The crusaders expected, quite reasonably under the circumstances, that the blind and newly restored emperor would be dependent on his son Alexios. It was the son who had promised to pay the crusaders a huge portion of the gold and coins in the empire's treasury for their assistance in restoring his father to the throne.

The amount of gold and coins promised to the crusaders was a sum so large that the crusaders had abandoned their vows to fight to liberate Jerusalem from the Saracens and, instead, had been transported to Constantinople by the Venetians to help restore the old emperor to the throne. They did so despite the pleas and excommunication threats of the Pope who wanted them to go to the Holy Land and reclaim Jerusalem from Saladin and his Saracens.

Indeed, Thomas, the brother of the archers' captain and now the Bishop of Cornwall, had travelled on an English galley to deliver the Pope's message—and had been betrayed and captured by the Venetians when he tried to deliver it. That's when the fighting between the Englishmen of the Company of Archers and the Venetians started once again—when Captain William and his English archers responded to Thomas's capture by attacking and capturing the galleys and cogs the Venetians were using to transport and supply their crusader allies.

Basically, the English archers, who were increasingly calling themselves Marines because they fight on both land and sea, began killing Venetians and taking their galley and transports—and continued to do so until Thomas was released at the "request" of the increasingly desperate and hungry crusaders.

Of course the crusaders demanded that Thomas be released— they knew about the English archers and feared they would be stranded without any transport to carry them home and sold into slavery. That's what William, the archers' captain and Thomas's brother, had promised would happen to the crusaders and their Venetian allies if his brother was not immediately released. He meant it and they knew it.

******

It all came about, the missing gold that is, when the then-current Greek emperor of the Byzantines, also confusingly named Alexios, had led his army out of the city to fight the outnumbered crusaders, perhaps in hopes they would turn and run and go back to their homes or off to Jerusalem as the Pope had been demanding.

The crusaders didn't run; they were willing to fight if that's what it would take to get the old emperor restored and themselves paid all of the gold and coins that his son had promised them for their assistance in restoring him.

When the crusaders didn't run, the emperor and his generals remembered what had happened the last time his army had come out to fight—when his army had marched out to confront a much smaller force of the English archers and been slaughtered by their longbows and their long pikes with hooks and blades.

As soon as he realised that there would actually be fighting, and particularly when he realised that he himself might be among those killed by the crusaders, the emperor led his army back inside Constantinople's walls—and ran away that very night with the gold in his treasury. He left on a galley manned, of all things, by the very same English archers who had earlier destroyed his useless navy and defeated his army. The English were, everyone including the fleeing emperor knew, quite reliable if they made their mark on a contract. That's why, of course, so many people paid such high prices for their services.

Many of the emperor's highest ranking courtiers also hired galleys crewed by William's English archers and escaped—each of them thinking that he and he alone had gotten away with the treasury's gold coins and bars. None of them had, of course, not even the emperor—although they probably don't know it yet because each still thought that he had gotten the gold and coins and carefully hidden them away.

In fact, they'd all been gulled by the former serf who had become the captain of the English archers, even the emperor himself. The emperor and his courtiers had each stolen away with, and carefully hidden, chests full of rocks; the gold itself had been taken by the Englishmen and ended up in Cornwall at the archers' base at Restormel Castle.

******

At first after the emperor and his courtiers fled everything proceeded as the crusaders and their Venetian allies had demanded—their demands had been fully met. The blind old man had been restored to the throne a few days after the emperor and his courtiers had run away on the English galleys with their sealed chests full of rocks that they thought were full of gold.

Then nothing happened, at least nothing good happened so far as the crusaders and Venetians were concerned. They weren't paid the gold coins and other valuables they'd been promised, and the restored emperor's son, the one who had made the agreement to pay the crusaders if his father was restored, was not even allowed to enter the city to help the blind old man govern.

After a few days of waiting in vain for the gold they'd been promised, the restless and increasingly hungry crusaders demanded that the blind emperor's son, the one who'd made his mark on the contract with them, be allowed to return to the city and named co-emperor "to help his father meet his obligations." To back up their demand, the leaders of the crusaders readied their men to move once again against the city in the event their demand for the gold they were owed was not met.

And once again the city's remaining decision makers both confounded and disappointed the crusaders and Venetians who had been looking for an excuse to sack the city—they agreed to the appointment of the son as a co-emperor. He immediately entered the city and joined his father on the throne.

Alexios, the son of the restored emperor and now co-emperor, was not stupid. He knew how weak the city's defenses had become from the years of corruption and neglect, and he also knew the strength of the crusaders and what would happen if they weren't paid—so the very first thing he did was send two of his most reliable men, cousins he'd met during his years of exile, to the treasury room to fetch the gold and pay the crusaders.

The two Greeks who had responded to the new co-emperor's orders to fetch the gold from the emperor's treasure room and deliver one thousand pounds of it to the crusaders hadn't been fools when they agreed to support the son of the emperor—they were ambitious and they were smart; they knew that the young Alexios would be the power behind the throne because his father was old and sick and blind.

They also know that the son promised much of the gold in the treasury to the crusaders if they would help him get his father out of prison and restore him to the throne. The promise had not been made, the two Greeks knew, because the son loved his father and wanted to see him back in his rightful place; it had been made so the son could inherit the throne from him.

It was a difficult, but not impossible, position that the two Greeks were in. They had been, and still were, among the son's most dedicated and loyal supporters—and rightly so; they were ambitious men and they hoped to get their hands on some of the gold for themselves. If they didn't, they planned to console themselves by being powerful officials in the son's empire and enriching themselves over time.

But where had all the gold gone and what should they do now? And who was to be the messenger who tells the emperor's waiting son, the new co-emperor, that it was missing? And what would the crusaders do when they found out there was no gold in the treasury to pay them? The choices of the two men are very basic—should they stay and risk the wrath of the crusaders and the hot-tempered and conniving new co-emperor, or should they run and save themselves?

******

The son's two courtiers were not the only ones with big troubles and significant decisions to make. The summer of 1203 was a difficult time for all the people living in one of the world's richest and largest cities—Constantinople, the glittering and cosmopolitan seat of the Greek Orthodox Church and the capitol city of the great and far flung Byzantine Empire.

Constantinople had been the capitol of the large and powerful Byzantine Empire and the seat of its emperor for almost a thousand years, ever since the division of the old Roman Empire into its western half oriented religiously towards Catholic Christian Rome and its Pope and its eastern half oriented religiously towards Orthodox Christian Constantinople and its Patriarch.

Much of the current trouble actually had its roots in something that had happened twenty years earlier. That's when the Orthodox Church and the recently restored blind emperor had encouraged the city's Greek-speaking residents to rise up and massacre the city's so-called "Latins"—those who looked to the Pope and the Latin speaking church in Rome for spiritual guidance instead of to the Orthodox Patriarch and Greek speaking church in Constantinople.

The "Latins," of course, being primarily the Venetians who had come to dominate the Orthodox empire's trade and finance. Throughout the empire the Venetians and other "Latins" who weren't killed by the irate Greeks and their subjects were sold to the Moors as slaves to help pay for the troubles they'd caused.

Elimination of the "Latins" throughout the empire should have settled things and been the end of the problems between the Orthodox Catholic Greeks and the Roman Catholic non-Greeks. But that turned out not to be the end of the conflict for several two reasons.

First, the Venetians were nothing if not great merchants and traders. And so, for that matter, were their traditional competitors, the Genoans and Pisans. The Venetians, in particular, had memories of the great profits they had reaped from the empire, and fought over with the Genoans and Pisans and others, before the empire's Greeks and other Orthodox Christians got fed up with their behaviour and threw them all out in the great massacre.

The potential profits were just too much to ignore—so slowly but surely the "Latins" returned to Constantinople and the other cities in its great empire. Even the Venetians began returning despite their great hatred of the Greeks and desire for revenge.

So twenty years later the priests and followers of both Christian religious organizations were once again living together inside the walls of the empire's biggest city and once again they were divided on what they considered to be very significant issues such as how one makes the sign of the cross and which priests were to receive the coins that the faithful pay to get relief from their sins and properly married and buried in the eyes of God.

On the other hand, the Venetians are still seriously pissed about what happened twenty years earlier. They wanted revenge, and no one more so than the Doge, the elderly ruler of Venice, who had only been able to grind his teeth in dismay when his people in far away Constantinople were massacred and enslaved twenty years earlier.

Venice was a maritime nation with a great navy and many transports and galleys. Twenty years ago, when the Venetians and the other "Latins" were massacred, Venice didn't have an army that its ruler could send to protect them or revenge their deaths. It still didn't—but now it has the crusaders.

******

Constantinople itself and the empire everyone wanted to rule and exploit were ancient. The city was consecrated in its present form by the Roman Emperor Constantine in the year 330AD. Constantine's heirs, or at least men claiming to be his heirs, have ruled it and adhered to the beliefs of the Orthodox Christian Church ever since.

Constantinople had everything—it was the rich, large, and powerful capitol of a huge and far flung empire of states and nations extending far out beyond its massive walls. The city's primarily Greek-speaking population was huge, five or six times that of London's—somewhere around one hundred and fifty thousand despite losing as many as fifty thousand people a few years earlier in the fighting when the "Latins" were massacred.

Even more important to the Greeks and everyone else who lives in the city—Constantinople was safe and secure from the threat of invasion and attack. It was safe and secure because it is built on a peninsula extending out into the Sea of Marmara and therefore protected on three sides by a great natural moat of water that comes right up to the city walls; on the fourth side it is protected by two huge and moated curtain walls with periodic defense towers.

Many invaders have tried to conquer the city and its empire over the centuries since Constantine had established it almost nine hundred years earlier; all had broken against the city's walls and failed. The city itself has been policed and defended under the leadership of the emperor's four thousand or so personal guards, the Varangians, for the past three hundred years or more.

The Varangians are the most dependable mercenaries of the day—loyal mercenaries from over sea—mainly Scandinavians including Norsemen displaced by the Anglo Saxons and Anglo Saxons displaced by the Normans. Collectively they are known as the axe bearers and they have a fearsome reputation.

We English archers, of course, have had our own problems with the city's imperial and religious leaders. A couple of years ago they kidnapped some of our archers and held them for ransom. Then last year the Venetians grabbed my priestly brother Thomas when he tried to deliver a papal letter to the crusaders after the Venetians had carried them to Constantinople so they could besiege the city.

Fortunately both times we archers were able to satisfactorily resolve our differences by acting like intelligent and reasonable men—we started killing the bastards, blockading the city, and taking their galleys and transports until they set our men free.

Today we have no complaints even though the Emperor and his courtiers and the Patriarch have just fled and sooner or later the city will probably fall to the crusaders and there will be no more coins to be earned by carrying refugees away to safety. Of course we have no complaints—we're on our way to Cornwall with both the refugee coins we'd already collected and the crates of gold coins and bars from the Byzantine treasury.

It's been a very good year.

Chapter Two
We return to Cornwall.

Tori and I returned to Cornwall from Constantinople early this afternoon to a warm and tumultuous welcome from our family—her two sisters who I'd also taken as wives and their howling infants, my priestly brother Thomas, and my son George. They all came to the river landing to greet us and so did many others.

Someone must have seen Harold's galley rowing its way up the river for they were all hurrying down the castle path towards us as Harold's sailors threw the mooring lines to the waiting hands of the men rapidly assembling around the little floating wharf tied to the trees on the side of the river.

As Tori and I rushed ashore to hug and kiss our family I quickly counted and breathed a sigh of relief without really realizing it. All three of the infant girls, Helen's two and Anne's one, had made it through the winter. I remember how sad Tori had been when she lost her little one last year.

Babies are such a scare and a joy and a dread aren't they? Now I understand why Helen's mother had pressed her owner to send Helen's sisters to me as well—so they can care for one another and keep me away from tavern girls and prostitutes who might pox me.

"Hoy, My Dears. It's good to see you."

And, of course, there was an especially warm welcome of hugs and back slaps from my son and heir.

"My God George, look at you— I swear you've grown a foot in these past months whilst I was gone. Good on you, son, good on you."

Then I looked over my shoulder and gave an important order.

"Harold, please have some of the men carry the chests to the hall." *George and I can carry them upstairs later.*

It was an order I needn't have given. I smiled and nodded an appreciative acknowledgement at Harold as soon as I looked over my shoulder as I was making it—for as the words came out of my mouth I turned and saw the chests with the gold from the emperor's treasury and the refugee coins already being unloaded on to our wharf and carried ashore.

Harold and I promptly beamed at each other. Harold's one of my five lieutenants, a good and loyal man and that's the all of it. Freeing him from being a galley slave when we bought our first galleys with the coins we took off the murdering bishop Thomas killed was one of the best moves Thomas and I ever made.

I can hardly wait to tell Thomas about all the gold we gulled off the Greeks. He'll be astonished. It certainly advances our plan for George, doesn't it? I'll tell him and George about it tonight when we're alone. A lot of people know we brought some coins and gold with us as we usually do; but only Harold and I know how much and about the gold.

******

We've been away for some time and my initial impression as we gathered together and talked was that we were continuing to grow and prosper.

If I understand correctly from what I heard as we walked up the cart path to the castle, the biggest change whilst I've been away is that Thomas and his assistant teacher, Ranulph, and the boys they've been learning now have their own hovel—they've moved out of the castle's great hall and taken over and improved the long shed in the bailey along the inside of the curtain wall between two of the inner wall's defensive towers. That's the shed which used to be used as the stables for the castle's horses.

The stables as I later came to find out have been moved to the much larger bailey inside the second curtain wall, the castle's outer wall.

Thomas's school is a long wattle and daub shed with

wooden shutters and a thatched roof running all along the west side of the outer wall below the ramparts. The boys are now sleeping and studying there instead of in the castle's hall.

"We put out a piss pot and dug a shite hole nearby and we're almost finished building a fireplace so it will be warm enough come winter. Next year we'll put slate on the roof so it won't catch fire if there is an accident or we are attacked."

Before I left Thomas and I had talked about him putting George and the other students in one or more of the towers of the inner curtain wall. Thomas said he decided against it because the towers are nowhere near large enough unless we split the boys up—which he does not want to do.

"I want them all together so the older boys can learn to be sergeants by sergeanting the young ones, and Ranulph and I can watch them all."

It was probably the best decision. The towers built into the wall are primarily bastions with arrow slits so archers can shoot at attackers trying to shelter against the wall while the attackers attempt to climb it or break through it. They're good fighting positions but they don't have much room where the boys can sleep and be learnt about the world and to scribe and gobble church talk.

Thomas has always wanted to keep the boys living and being learnt together with himself and Ranulph nearby so they can keep an eye on them—and now, Thomas informed me with a great deal of satisfaction as we walked up the cart path, they are all living and being learnt together even though there are more of them.

He and Ranulph are each living in one of the towers of the inner curtain wall with the school running all along the inside of wall between them.

Harold and Peter have the other two towers at the corners of the castle's inner wall whilst Raymond and the other senior sergeants posted to Restormel and their women share the seven shorter towers of the outer wall. The archers and their chosen men and file sergeants, and the castle's horses, are in the sheds and stables that run all the way around the inside of the outer curtain wall.

Our unpaid apprentice archers, of course, are still in their tents outside the second wall; the servants and workers are in the various hovels they've erected for themselves outside the partially finished third wall of which only one section is complete.

Our servants and workers don't know it yet, but in the years ahead they may end up having to move their hovels—we've already decided to build a fourth wall when the third curtain wall is finished and also to install apron walls to divide each of the baileys into defensible sections. A home with families and coins to protect can never be too strong these days and we've got to keep the men busy, don't we?

****** *William*

Supper that evening in the castle hall was a happy and boisterous occasion with my excited women chattering away, infant children howling, boys playing, and George sitting next to me listening to the men talk and trying to act like a grown up. It was a homecoming celebration so we used three candles to light the hall up. The younger boys in Thomas's school used their hands and fingers to make shadow figures on the wall whilst the adults talked and the older boys listened.

Later that evening my brother and I were able to learn each other a lot when things quieted down and we finally had a chance to talk privately. Much has happened since we both left Cornwall last autumn—me to go to the Holy Land and end up coming home with the emperor's gold; Thomas and Peter to go to Rome to pay the Pope his share of the passengers' prayer donations and being asked to help deliver a papal message to the crusaders.

Delivering the Pope's message, of course, is how Thomas ended up getting captured last year by the damn Venetians—they grabbed him because they didn't want it delivered.

The sun had long ago gone down and everyone else had gone off to their beds when we sat together, just the three of us, at the table in the hall. It was time for my brother and me to bring each other up to date by talking about our men and galleys, about Constantinople and Rome, and about the crusaders and Venetians and everything else.

George sat with us to listen and learn so we talked about everything except certain personal matters and other things that are best left unsaid with a young boy present even if he is approaching manhood. *And approaching it rather nicely if I do say so myself.*

We had much to talk about. It's been a couple of months since I led the raid on the Venetian shipping that resulted in my priestly brother being released by the Venetians and hurrying home. Unfortunately, Thomas left Constantinople so quickly to return to Cornwall and his students after the Venetians freed him that we didn't have much time to talk.

Before he left Thomas had tried to explain what had happened why the Venetians grabbed him. I didn't really learn very much when Thomas was freed because he immediately left for Cornwall. Moreover, at the time I was distracted—first by the need to bring in men and galleys to cope with the flood of rich refugees coming out of Constantinople, and then by the lure of the gold bars and the coins and jewels the emperor and his various officials were trying to remove from the Byzantine treasury and take with them as they fled.

Now that I was finally back in Cornwall, Thomas was once again trying to explain what caused him and some of our men to be captured by the crusaders and Venetians when he tried to deliver the Pope's letter. It's something we're overdue to talk about—there was a lot I needed to know, particularly since I'll be turning around and going right back out to Constantinople again in a couple of weeks.

"There is no question about it," I assured Thomas with a nod of agreement and a serious look on my face. "If I'm going to make good decisions out there I need to know more about all sorts of things." *I said that about my having to know many things to make good decisions to help learn George; my brother understood what I was doing and nodded his appreciation as I continued.*

"So let me tell you what I know about what happened and why I think it happened.

"For me the situation between the Greeks and the crusaders is still a bit confusing. But I certainly understand more than I did a couple of years ago when the Greeks grabbed some of our men and wanted us to pay a ransom to free them. As I'm sure your remember, that was when we replied to the Greeks' ransom demands by making the emperor and his courtiers a counter offer they didn't dare refuse—you free our men and we'll stop taking your galleys and killing your men.

"As you might also remember, we responded to the Greeks' ransom demands by attacking their wormy old fleet where it was anchored next to the city's walls and fighting off an attack by their sad excuse for an army. To this day I wonder if we could have taken the city. But the Greeks quickly freed our men and gave us a small parcel of land outside the wall and a quay to use for a trading concession so I guess we'll never find out."

"After that, everything went smoothly for us for a while until the Venetians brought the crusaders to the city instead of taking them to the Holy Land—and grabbed you when you tried to deliver the Pope's message threatening the crusaders with excommunication if they attacked the city."

Then I told my brother and son all about how we attacked the Venetians until they freed Thomas and how I got the gold when the emperor and his courtiers fled after Thomas left to go back to England. They could hardly believe it and laughed heartily when I told them how I gulled the Greeks and ended up with the emperor's gold by moving the chests back and forth under their very eyes until we had the chests with filled with gold and they had the chests filled with stones.

"Twenty five chests?" Thomas exclaimed. "My God, William, those chests are heavy. I helped carry a couple of them up the stairs myself and it was all I could do to lift them by myself. They must hold at least a couple of thousand pounds of gold and silver; maybe more, by God."

Then I laughed to myself and told Thomas and George more of the details of how I'd done it and who had helped and why the emperor and some of his officials probably still think they've succeeded in getting the gold for themselves and hiding it away.

What I didn't mention to Thomas and George, and never will, is the truth—that the only reason the emperor and his courtiers didn't succeed in carrying the gold away for themselves was because the temptation for me to steal it for myself was just too great to overcome. All Thomas and George know is that I gulled Greeks and took it— and so far no one even seems to know the gold is gone, let alone who actually has it.

"It all started, the taking of the gold that is, when we were paid handsomely to have some of our galleys stand by to carry the emperor and some of his priests and courtiers to safety in the event they decided to flee the city.

"That was in the early days right after the Venetians brought the crusaders from Zara and began their siege of Constantinople—and, sure enough, the emperor and his high-ranking courtiers and churchmen fled. That happened right after the emperor led his army out to fight the crusaders and then turned around and scurried back behind his walls when he realised that people get killed when armies fight and that he himself might be one of them.

"The Greeks had earlier come to us and made their marks on the contracts wherein they gave us a goodly amount of coins and we agreed to have galleys standing by to carry the emperor and some of his courtiers away to safety if they ever so requested. Just passengers, mind you, that's all we contracted to carry.

"Unfortunately for the emperor and his fellow thieves, they didn't want us to know they were stealing the gold so not a single one of the contracts on which we all made our marks obliged us to carry or protect anything else except our passengers—so we didn't."

Then I spent quite some time telling my brother and my son the details of how we moved the gold chests back and forth through the little window we made in one of the galley's inside walls—and over and over again gulled the various Greeks by substituting chests full of rocks for those with all the gold.

I embellished the tale and had both of them laughing with delight as I described how each of the Greeks sent a man down to get the gold chests out of the galley's specially constructed little hold—and he couldn't get them out because the ladder he needed to stand on was in the way. So the only possible solution was to have a strong and very tall archer go down into the hold by himself and lift them out, someone so tall he didn't need to stand on a ladder.

"So far we seem to have gotten away with it. We carried the emperor and each of our other distinguished escaping passengers safely away from the city and each thinks he has safely hidden the gold chests away where no one else can find them. In fact each hid chests full of stones; the chests with the gold and coins are all right here in Cornwall at this very moment—upstairs with the rest of our coin chests as a matter of fact."

Thomas put down his bowl of ale and looked at George quite seriously.

"There are a lot of lessons for you in what your father just told us, George," Thomas admonished my wide eyed and smiling son and heir when I finished and took a big slurp of ale from my bowl.

"Absolutely never ever abandon your men; get all the information you can before you make your decisions; consider the future not just today; honour your contracts to keep your reputation and attract future custom; never give in to blackmail; and be smart when you seize your opportunities—and never trust Greeks and Venetians."

God, I hope my son looks up to me and Thomas is learning him good. Now I need to take a piss before it's Thomas's turn to talk.

******

Thomas is my priestly brother and he's usually right when he suggests something—so after I came back from pissing I dipped myself another bowl of ale out of the barrel by the fireplace, put both elbows on the table, and settled in to listen with George once again at my side.

According to what Thomas began explaining to us, it all started about twenty years ago when Constantinople's Roman Catholic population was removed from the city in a "great massacre of the Latins," meaning primarily the Venetians who had come to dominate most of the Byzantine empire's maritime and financial trade.

The last straw for the Greeks and their emperor came when the Venetians began openly fighting with the Genoans and Pisans and other Latins living in the city to get control of the rest of the empire's affairs—and at the same time committed the unpardonable sin of bringing in their own priests to perform their ceremonies and collect the tithes and fees and donations generated by the Christian churches.

"The Greeks killed them all, didn't they? Almost everyone in the city whose priests prayed in Latin was slaughtered. Tens of thousands of good Roman Catholics fell, almost all of them Venetians—except three or four thousand women and children the emperor sold to the Moors as slaves.

"As you might imagine, George, killing off just about all the Venetians and selling some of their women and children into slavery greatly upset Venice and the Venetians. They've been trying to get revenge on the Greeks and their empire ever since.

"For a while everything went along fairly smoothly in the Greeks' empire after the massacre—until the emperor in Constantinople was overthrown and replaced by his brother. Allegedly it happened in response to the corruption and financial extravagance of the emperor and his courtiers.

"He was overthrown by his own brother, Alexios, who promptly seized his brother's wealth and women and replaced his brother's courtiers with his own. But the new emperor made a serious mistake—he merely blinded and sent his deposed older brother off to prison.

"Blinding instead of killing his older brother when he deposed him was a serious mistake and it came back to haunt Alexios years later when the deposed emperor's son joined up with the crusaders and some of his father's old supporters to try to restore his father to the throne.

"Efforts to restore the old and blinded emperor didn't happen immediately, of course. At first everything continued to go along fairly smoothly for the new emperor, meaning the emperor's Varangian Guards were paid their wages and the corruption and mismanagement continued to the satisfaction of the new emperor's courtiers.

"That relative calm lasted for almost twenty years— until a couple of years ago when some of the new emperor's courtiers ran out of money and began trying to raise new money—by grabbing people visiting and working in Constantinople, particularly foreigners, and holding them for ransom." *And chopping off their heads if their families and overlords didn't pay.*

"Things began to change when a couple of the emperor's courtiers made the mistake of grabbing some of our archers who were in Constantinople operating our trading post. The emperor and his courtiers thought Englishmen, being as we look to the Pope in Rome for our priests and prayers the same as the Venetians and other Italians do, were like them and so would be willing to pay a ransom to regain our men's freedom just as some of the Latins did twenty years ago to avoid being sold into slavery.

"That was a bad mistake the Greek's made, George, thinking we English were like the Venetians and other Italians—instead of paying the ransom they demanded, your father and our archers promptly destroyed a good portion of the emperor's wormy and useless fleet—and forced him to free our men and give us payments and additional concessions to stop your father from continuing his attacks on the city and its navy and transports. We also kept the emperor's wormy galleys even though they were virtually worthless because of their sad condition.

"Then last year something important happened—the son of the blinded and imprisoned former emperor met Boniface, the Italian who became the leader of the crusaders after their first leader died. It was a significant meeting because the son of the former emperor promised the crusaders all the gold coins and bars in the empire's treasury if they would go to Constantinople and help his father regain his throne instead of going to the Holy Land to fight the Saracens and regain Jerusalem.

"The riches on offer were too great to turn down—the crusaders agreed to help restore the old emperor and the Venetians not only cheerfully carried them to Constantinople to intimidate the Greeks, but also sent what few troops Venice had to join them."

"The Venetians were happy to do it because they hate the Byzantines so much; the crusaders agreed because they wanted the empire's great riches promised by the old emperor's son.

"That, of course, is when Pope again tried to stop the crusaders and get them off to the Holy Land where they belong. I got involved by trying to help deliver the Pope's letter that ordered the crusaders to go to the Holy Land and fight Saracens instead of going to Constantinople to fight Christians—and the Venetians grabbed me to stop its delivery.

"They didn't hold me for long. Your father and our men immediately began pressing the Venetians to release me by taking their galleys as prizes and promising to keep taking more and more of them until I was free. So they released me and the crusaders got the letter from the Pope—and promptly decided to ignore it because going to Constantinople to restore the old emperor promised much greater riches and rewards than regaining Jerusalem and the lands around it could ever possibly provide.

"The rest is history—the crusaders started to attack Constantinople and scared the emperor so much that he deserted his post and his people and tried to escape with all the gold bars and coins and jewels in the Greek treasury— the gold and coins and jewels you and your father and Harold and I carried upstairs earlier today."

Then Thomas took a big gulp of ale from his bowl and looked at me in the flickering light of the candle lamp.

"Well William, that's what I learned when they held me prisoner. What do I need to know if something happens to you? Did you learn anything else after I left?"

"Not much, Thomas, not much at all; except that the Greeks are like the Venetians and crusaders and our own priests and nobles—they can't be trusted. They are also too smart by half and don't have much of a bottom for a fight."

I said it with a laugh after I took a big swallow of ale

from my own bowl. Then I tried to fill in some of the gaps by explaining what I had learned.

"After Emperor Alexios and the gold disappeared the city's leaders immediately did exactly as the crusaders demanded and restored his blinded brother Issac to the throne—but the Byzantine army still wouldn't let the emperor's son or the crusaders into the city, at least they hadn't let them in by the time I sailed for Cornwall with the emperor's gold.

"I didn't wait around after the emperor and his courtiers ran away thinking they had the gold, so maybe things have changed. But when I left to bring the gold here the crusaders were still outside the city's walls and seemed befuddled and quite angry about not being paid. They didn't know what to do next now that their initial demand to restore the old emperor had been fully met."

"Well Brother William," Thomas said with a smile as he playfully mussed my son's hair and took a sip of ale, "the crusaders and the emperor's son may have gotten the emperor they wanted released from prison and restored the poor blind old bastard to the throne, but they didn't get into the city and they certainly didn't get their hands on the gold or get control of the city's treasury and its empire. I wonder what they'll do now? What do you think?"

"Damned if I know. But what I think is I'd better go piss again and it's time for George to get some sleep." *And me too; I'm tired.*

****** *William*

Three days later we learned a lot more. One of our

galleys, the galley captained by Jeffrey, the archer who used to be a brewer's apprentice in York, came in from Constantinople with a report. The crusaders are now demanding that the son of the restored emperor be made co-emperor.

The crusaders are obviously doing so, of course, so the emperor's son can get the gold they think is in the treasury and use it to pay them. According to the message from Martin, the archer who is the senior sergeant captaining our post in Constantinople, the city's leaders and the Orthodox Patriarch refused to agree to a co-emperor and the crusaders are once again preparing to lay siege to the city and sack it.

Two days later another galley came in from the east with another message from Constantinople. The city's leaders have changed their minds and given in to avoid a war—they have agreed to make the blind emperor's son up to be the co-emperor and let him enter the city.

"Well," said Thomas with a wry smile, "If the emperor's son didn't know the treasury was empty before this, he certainly knows now that he's in the city. I wonder how soon he'll tell the crusaders and what they'll do when they find out they won't be paid?"

"I don't know what the crusaders will do to Constantinople but I don't think the fact that the gold is missing will come back to hurt us," I replied.

"Everyone who knows the treasury is empty probably thinks they know exactly what had happened to the gold— the fleeing emperor and his courtiers took it with them when they fled on the galleys they contracted from us."

After I thought about things for a few seconds I added a bit more to my answer.

"There were several hundred people on each of our galleys so sooner or later, of course, everyone will know that we carried the fleeing Greeks and that our galleys stopped and waited whilst they took their crates of gold ashore and hid them. Hopefully they will also learn that our men deliberately stayed on board so they wouldn't have a clue as to where the crates were hidden.

"But you're right, Thomas,—the two big questions are what will the crusaders do when they find out the treasury is empty? And has anyone even told them the gold is gone or is it still a big secret?"

Chapter Three
Return to the Holy Land.

Supping on my last night at home was entirely a family affair. My lieutenants and Thomas's boys and Ranulph who helps Thomas put the learning on the boys in his school were not there. My son George, of course, was present along with my brother Thomas and the three sisters who are George's stepmothers and all three of our infants—all little girls with red hair just like their two mothers'.

The irrepressible Tori was finally back from her dark days after she lost her little girl to the pox last year. Accompanying me on the trip to Constantinople worked wonders for her and, truth be told, for me too. *If you ever have to take a sea voyage try to bring a woman with you. You can keep her busy rubbing your back and doing other things to please you.*

Ever since we returned Tori's been regaling her two sisters with stories about our trip and the places and markets she visited and the people we met, some of them wildly funny and made up in part from her imagination. She desperately wants another baby, at least that's what Helen told me when she came to my bed last night—so would I please take her sister with me when I go back to Constantinople tomorrow?

It was easy to agree—I knew Helen and Anne couldn't come with me because they're still nursing our infants and it's well known that bouncing around on the ocean curdles the milk in a mother's breasts. I'd already made up my mind that I wanted Tori to come with me. So I admitted to Helen that in the morning I intended to announce that Tori would be going with me. *It's strange isn't it—as I get older I like my warmth and comforts and appreciate them even more.*

What I didn't expect was Helen's squeal of joy at the news and her jumping out of bed totally naked to run to tell Tori that she would be sailing with me—and the celebration that the news generated among the three sisters.

"Of course we're happy; we don't want you finding someone else to care for you," Helen whispered into my ear when she came back to bed after much squealing, giggling, and whispering with her sisters.

So now everyone knows—Tori is coming with me when I return to Cyprus and Constantinople today on Harold's galley. So is one of my Lieutenants, Peter

Sergeant who fought so well at Launceston and elsewhere. Two other galleys will be sailing with us. We'll use candle lanterns to stay together as long as possible and then, as we always do, rendezvous at various ports along the way

Harold's galley is crewed with over one hundred and forty of our best archers and sailors; the other two galleys will be carrying a little over a hundred of our newly trained archers, their veteran sergeants and chosen men, and about three dozen or so passengers who have been accumulating in Fowey Village since our last sailing. We'll also be carrying and some parchment letters and money orders that came in from our trading post in London on behalf of various London merchants.

We have no raids or cutting out expeditions planned for along the way, but if we are fortunate enough to see any Moorish galleys or transports we'll certainly try to take them. Harold's superb galley with its crew of experienced sailors and two veteran archers with longbows and either bladed pikes or swords at every oar is arguably the fastest and most powerful warship that ever sailed.

******

Gary's and Alan's galleys had already cast off and begun floating down the river to Fowey village to pick up their passengers when Harold's galley was pulled up to our floating wharf for loading. The other two galleys will pick up their passengers whilst we are loading and wait for us at the mouth of the River Fowey where it comes into the channel at the head of the estuary.

Quite a large group of people came to see us off—

George, his stepmothers and our children, and, of course, my priestly brother Thomas and his students. George doesn't know it, but Thomas and I seriously discussed my taking him and Thomas's five oldest students with me on this trip. They're almost old enough. Next year they'll be ready to spread their wings for sure.

Our departure involved the usual chaotic loading of supplies including water, firewood, recently taken hinds, and squawking chickens, bleating sheep, and bawling cattle—all nobbled, of course, so they can't rush around the deck and do damage if they somehow get loose.

Finally Harold finished yet another inspection of his galley and nodded his satisfaction. All is ready; it was time to go.

Big last minute hugs and kisses for everyone and the mooring lines were cast off. Tori and I waved and smiled at our family and friends until we drifted around the bend in the river and out of sight beyond the trees. I found myself strangely anxious to be on my way.

Our companion galleys will fall in with us as we row out of the River Fowey's mouth and head towards our first rendezvous at the Portuguese port of Oporto. From there we'll travel along the coast to Lisbon and then make the long run past Gibraltar to Palma on the island of Mallorca and then to Malta.

After Malta, Peter and I and Tori will head north on Harold's galley to Piraeus and Constantinople accompanied by one of our companion galleys; the other galley, probably Alan's, will continue on to Crete and Cyprus with the passengers and parchments contracted for the Holy Land

and its ports.

Our passengers are a motley bunch who reached Cornwall on one or another of our galleys and cogs coming in from London and elsewhere. They have been accumulating at the ale house in Fowey Village whilst waiting for our next sailing to Cyprus and the Holy Land.

Fowey is where our London galleys and cogs and those coming from Liverpool and France drop their outbound passengers. It's a poor and tiny village of fishermen with only one sparse alehouse and an old church which has no priest. Only our recruits who have signed with the company to be apprentice archers are taken all the way up the Fowey to the castle and our big training camp.

The training camp is where we feed our new recruits, learn them to use swords and walk together on the same foot, and try to strengthen their arms enough to push an arrow out of a longbow.

Today's passengers include a couple of Hospitallers en route to Acre via Cyprus, a dozen or so pilgrims led by a priest from York who are also bound for Acre as their last stop before proceeding on to Jerusalem, four young aspirants from Yorkshire who hope to become Hospitallers, and a dozen or more merchants bound for Lisbon and the intermediate ports where we usually stop further along the way.

There is also a rather large gaggle of priests and monks and three older men of uncertain origin who appear to be fleeing felons or debtors. Everyone's welcome if they've got enough coins, are willing to help with the rowing, and behave themselves.

******

We were able to use the candle lanterns on our masts to stay together all the way to Oporto. We came into the Oporto harbour one right after another and moored our galleys at the same quay. Then we did the usual—took on water and supplies and made sure each of our men got at least two hours of shore leave to drink a bowl of wine dip his dingle into a woman at one of the several harbour taverns along the road in front of the quay.

Tori and I and Peter walked on a narrow cobblestoned street to the city's market with small guard of half a dozen archers whilst Harold was seeing to the resupply of his galley and the others as well.

The street we walked was similar to the streets and lanes of London with shops on the street and sleeping rooms above them. If there was a difference it was that in Oporto none of the sleeping rooms above the merchants' shops extended out into the street to block the sun and hold off the rain.

Oporto's cobblestoned market was quite large and was crowded with people shoulder to shoulder, some shopping and others out for an evening stroll to greet their friends. They were walking in both directions in the shade provided by the walls and roofs of the market's shops and stalls.

The market's narrow lanes and market stalls were surprisingly crowded with people of all types and ages and dress from beggars to elegant ladies being carried in sedan chairs. Perhaps the crowds were so large because it was late in the day before night falls and the streets and market lanes were everywhere shaded because the sun had gone down enough that is direct shine was blocked by the market stalls.

All in all, Oporto was quite comfortable and felt quite safe. Even so, I wore my battered old chain mail shirt as I always do when I'm ashore and I was wearing my wrist knives under my tunic. The archers acting as our guards had their bows strung and their swords and axes ready.

Foreigners and sailors from cargo transports and galleys are two a penny here; despite our half dozen accompanying guards and their swords and strung bows, the only attention we attracted was from merchants who called out to us in the hope we might have coins and buy something.

Tori hadn't been to a proper market for several months so she made the most of it. It was enjoyable to watch her shop and the archers with us as our guards were quite taken by the pleasure she took in picking out things to buy and dealing with the merchants. They eagerly vied with one another to help carry her purchases.

******

There are taverns and merchants selling things to eat throughout the Oporto market. When Tori finally announced she was getting tired and had finished shopping we went into one of the taverns in the market for a drink of wine and a meal for everyone in our party.

What she confided to me with a most serious look on her face as we entered the tavern caused me to break into uproarious laughter and give her a big hug.

"I'm saving myself for the market in Lisbon; it's bigger don't you know?"

Tori's joy seemed to infuse the spirit of everyone around us, even those who hadn't heard her. We marched into the nearest tavern with big smiles on every face.

Our archer guards were quite pleased to join us and we all sat on benches ranged along one of the long wooden tables that filled the place from end to end. It was quite cool and pleasant with the flickering light of the dying sun beaming through the window openings and the two lanterns hanging from a ceiling beam. The archers were all heavily bearded long serving veterans with at least two stripes and had long experience ordering drinks and food in foreign taverns.

The archers laughed and pointed and talked too loud when they tried to make the serving girls understand what they wanted—it wasn't hard; the girls were quite pleasant and seemed to know a few words of every language.

In the end we returned to the ship with full stomachs and smiling archers cheerfully carrying a pillow, little coats for the three infant girls which "they will grow into, of course," some kind of women's dresses for Tori's sisters and fur shoes to keep their feet warm, and a carved wooden charm guaranteed to bring good fortune to women sailing towards the east.

Our cheerful return and an hour or two on land seemed to have a good effect on everyone. It was a happy galley when we cast off with favourable winds that evening and sailed out of the harbour in the moonlight. To Harold's great amazement it appeared that not a man of his crew or the other galleys had run. The only one who didn't return was one of the older merchants who had been seasick all the way to Oporto.

******

Our archers were practicing archery on deck and we were getting close to Lisbon when our lookout's hail alerted everyone that there is a sail in the distance on our starboard side—and then a minute or so later he shouted down that something didn't look right. It was dead in the water.

Harold shouted the necessary orders to the rudder men, sail men, and the rowing sergeant, and we altered course to look. It was a welcome diversion to a boring day. Our sister galleys followed us as we rowed towards it.

We closed on the distant ship fast as our rowing drum stepped up its beat and the new course put the wind full into our sails. As we got closer we could see that our lookout had a good eye—the cog we approached appeared deserted and was down in the water and moving erratically in response to the wind and the waves.

Our sailing sergeant put us deftly alongside the hulk and the grapples were thrown. Willing and curious hands quickly pulled us tight against her. Harold and I were standing on the roof of the stern castle. That's where we were when we first saw the dead man on the deck that the lookout had reported seeing a few minutes earlier.

Seeing the dead man on the deck caused Harold to tell the boarding party to hold back, to stay aboard whilst he climbed the mast get a better look.

"Either pirates or a pox," was Harold's comment as he

came down the mast and stood next to me along the deck railing. "I didn't see any blood or damage so it could well be a pox."

Everyone not at the oars was gathered on deck looking as we bobbed up and down next to the deserted cog.

Suddenly Harold roared. "Cast off your lines. Peeps, keep us upwind for sure. It's poxed and there's no way we can salvage it."

There was a scurry of activity—and then a problem. One of our grapples could not be shaken loose. Even a swearing and red faced Harold couldn't shake it free when he took over from the sailor who'd thrown it.

"Cut the goddamn line," a disgusted Harold finally ordered. In the background on the other side of the deck an elderly priest among our passengers nodded his approval at Harold's caution and a young one seethed at hearing the lord's name taken in vain.

******

"Anchor in the roads when you reach Lisbon. We'll rendezvous there. Don't tie up at any of the wharves or quays or let any of your men go ashore until we know if the city's poxed."

That was the order Harold shouted over the water to Gary and Alan, the sergeant captains of our other two galleys, immediately after we drew away from lifeless hulk. It's a good thing he gave the order immediately—the next morning only one of our two companion galleys was in sight, Gary's. We'd lost contact with Alan's galley during last night's wind and heavy rain.

"We need water but we've got enough food to go on to Faro if Lisbon is poxed, maybe even farther. Last I heard Faro was still in Christian hands. There's a little river where we can put in for water about half a day south of here."

******

We waited offshore for the sun to rise and then approached Lisbon carefully. Both of the other two galleys were waiting outside the harbour when the sun came up so we entered together.

Everything appeared normal as we approached the quay. Two harbour wharfies came over to grab the mooring lines as we approached.

"Is there sickness in the city?" Harold shouted. "Is the city poxed?"

The answer came in a language I could not understand and neither could Harold. Finally Harold shouted an order for a sailor to report to the mast; supposedly he knows how to speak Lisbon's strange Spanish dialect. According to Harold, it's sort of like Spanish but different.

A few minutes later the sailor who could speak the local language and a couple of volunteers pulled themselves up on to the old stone quay and went ashore. They returned in less than an hour to report that the merchants said the city was safe to enter—and with two of the city's officials in tow. Their inquiries had caused concern.

Harold and I had to argue with the local officials to get our men ashore. Finally common sense and a generous bribe prevailed and the officials agreed to let us come ashore. We motioned to the other two galleys waiting nearby to come to the quay and tie up. The numbers and calls of the sea gulls gathering overhead increased and increased as they did.

It's a pity we don't have someone here we could rely on to meet us and inform us about conditions here. Perhaps things will be different in the future and we'll have our own men who can come to the quay to greet us and keep the port officials sweet. For the past several years we've been talking about Lisbon's growing importance to us as a source of passengers and parchment money orders—so we hope to establish a shipping depot here as early as next year. We'll do it, that is, if we can find the right place to locate it near the harbour and the right man to be the post sergeant.

At the moment the plan is for Thomas to stop here and look for a place for a depot next year on his way to pay the Pope his share of the take from the passengers' prayer donations.

Jeffrey and Alan are both getting a bit long in the tooth so perhaps one of them would like to give up captaining his galley to sergeant the Lisbon post. Once again the big problem will be to find a dependable man who can scribe and sum to assist whomever is selected.

Hmm. Or perhaps one of them could take Randolph's place and he could come here. As always, there are never enough good men who can scribe and sum. That, of course, is why Thomas is putting so much learning on George and the boys.

******

Lisbon's huge central market is an absolute wonder and absolutely packed with people and goods to buy. Only Constantinople's great market is larger and more complete. Just about anything one might want to buy is available from weapons and linen and bags of corn for grinding, to sturdy men and comely young girls and boys.

Many things make the Lisbon market great in addition to its size and the variety of selections offered by its merchants. One important thing on a hot summer's day such as today is the tiled roof over each of the narrow lanes that runs between the market stalls separated from one another by wooden and stone walls.

Tori has been here twice before and it's obviously her favourite place in the entire world. She was so excited when we finally climbed off the galley that even the grizzled old archers who came along to be our guards were smiling. It seems she and her sisters had come up with a long list of linen for clothes and other things to buy to make living in Restormel more comfortable for themselves and our children; it was a very long list indeed.

Archers are almost always present when we go to markets and meetings and I always wear my chain shirt and carry my wrist knives. It's not that Harold and Peter and I expect trouble, to the contrary; but we're English and can never be too careful—our archers have killed a lot of men who needed killing and taken a lot of prizes. We may be respected and trusted and feared just about everywhere but we are far from being loved by everyone. Even pirates and thieves have families and friends.

We spent two entire days in the Lisbon market and it wasn't just Tori who bought things and asked questions. I visited the weapons and ironmongers stalls and on the second day of our visit I placed and partially paid for a huge order of armour piercing iron arrowheads, both "longs" and "heavies," to be delivered to both Cornwall and Cyprus.

On the same day at other merchants I also made my mark on test orders for metal pike tips, not the very long round wooden poles and bladed metal hooks mind you, just the metal tips. Our blacksmiths on Cyprus and in Cornwall will get the wood for the poles locally and add the bladed hooks to them separately.

I didn't buy the poles and bladed hooks because Henry, one of my five lieutenants and the one charged with training and equipping our men to fight on land, was adamant that we not buy all the parts of our bladed pikes in one market and never in England or France.

For as long as possible Henry wants to keep everyone we might have to fight in the dark about the long handled spears we started making and modifying on Cyprus and now also make in Cornwall—the ones we found to be so effective both in stopping charging knights and pulling and chopping the few who get past our pikes off their horses.

The archers have taken to calling them "horse pikes" because they can use them to take a toll on mounted attackers whether they're coming towards them or going past in the other direction. They can also be used to hold off men on foot and chop down on their heads.

Chapter Four

Horses at sea.

Our three galleys were heavily laden with supplies as we rowed out of Lisbon's harbour on the morning tide. The little castle in the bow which once seemed so large was now crowded with Tori's purchases of things that she and her sisters and "our dear little children" absolutely must have—piles of linen that can be cut and sewn to make clothes, and sandals, combs, mirrors, bedding, wooden chests, cooking spices, a bigger string bed, and a large and surprisingly pricey stack of brightly coloured carpets "to keep everyone's feet warm."

Peter and the archers who'd accompanied our trips to the market had desperately tried to keep smiles off their faces when I took Tori by the arm and quietly tried to explain to her that we could get some or all of these things when we stopped here on the way back to Cornwall or whilst we are in Constantinople.

My effort fell on deaf ears. Tori left me speechless for a second when she put her hands on her hips, leaned forward, and threw my own words back at me with grim determination and a keen look—"get it whilst you can; you never know if you'll have another chance; that's what *you* always say."

"You've been defeated and undone."

That was Peter's laughing comment and the watching archers roared when I opened my mouth to respond, and then closed it a moment later and ruefully nodded my agreement. I couldn't help myself; I started laughing too and so did Tori.

It was a delightful two days and every so often one of our guards carried another armload of Tori's "necessities" back to the galley's forecastle. We ate every meal in the market and twice she returned to the lane of spice stalls to buy a spice that had flavoured our food.

******

We lost sight of our two sister galleys even before the sun went down on our first day out of Lisbon. An Atlantic storm had just passed through and the sea was rough and the wind variable. Even Tori was affected. We both hung our heads over the side and used the shite pot instead of climbing out on to the nest hanging over the stern. It was so rough that even the archers' required daily archery and sword fighting practices were temporarily suspended.

Everything changed and spirits rose when we rowed past Gibraltar and into the Mediterranean. The winds turned favourable and the weather became warm and beautiful with puffy white clouds in a clear blue sky.

Harold stopped the rowing to rest the men and let the wind carry us. It wasn't long before some of the men were fishing off the stern and others were once again doing what they called "moors dancing" on the galley's main deck. Harold encourages both activities and makes sure all his captains allow them.

"It keeps them busy and out of mischief, doesn't it?"

Moors dancing involved eight to ten men standing in circles and squares and doing intricate steps and moves to the beat of the drum and the leader's calls. It involves periodic foot stampings, hand clappings, leg slappings, and arrow clickings as each man stamps and claps and slaps and whirls around and periodically taps his arrow against an arrow held by another man.

I remember watching moors dancing from my days as a village lad. Other than drinking when ale was available and chasing after the women, it was really all the men in the village had to do to entertain themselves. Each village had its own special set of dances and steps and the men and older boys danced them almost every Sunday after church even if it was raining.

Village dancers didn't use arrows, of course, just a dried stick pulled from a tree with its bark stripped off. Sometimes the men would walk to another village after church, or their men would come to ours, and there would be a contest to see who could dance the most intricate dances without missing a step.

On our galleys we sometimes have contests between different groups of men in our galley crews. Harold and I do the judging of the winners—when we aren't dancing ourselves even though we both do it rather badly compared to most of the men.

I enjoy moors dancing. I was just starting to learn the steps and moves for my village's dances when me mum died and Thomas came from the monastery to take me crusading and learn me how to scribe and be an archer.

It pains me to admit it, and of course I never will, but the sailors seem to be better dancers than the archers.

******

"Hoy the deck. Sails to the east by the north."

A few minutes later both Harold and I had finished climbing the mast to see for ourselves. There is no question about it—there are a large number of sails ahead of us and off to our starboard side. All kinds of sails and lots of them.

"Lieutenant," I said to Harold formally, "I'd be obliged if you'd take us around to get upwind from them. And please have the men standby to string their bows."

"At your orders, Captain," was Harold's loud and prompt response and he began giving orders. "Upwind it is; and stand by to string bows." *My good friend and I went formal because we may be getting ready to take our men into action. The men standing near us picked up on it instantly.*

"Blow the alert horn," roared Harold. "Rowing sergeant, pick up the beat to full; rudder man and sailing sergeant change course to due west. Standby to string bows. Arrow party to lay out and open the bales."

There was a perceptible stirring and murmur of voices throughout ship and almost instantly from the stern came five short toots from the ship's horn blower followed after a brief pause by five more. *The horn toots made it an official alert and it came fast as it should have done—the archer two striper who is the horn man carries his horn at all times on a leather strap around his neck.*

Immediate loud commands began to be given by various sergeants. The men who'd been idling at the water skin dashed for their rowing seats, sailors rushed to begin working on the rigging to lower the sail so we could head west into the wind, the designated archer lookouts grabbed their bows and began scrambling up the mast, and the cook stopped frying flat bread and began dousing his fire with water from his nearby leather bucket.

Our galley heeled over a bit as we made a tight turn to starboard and our speed began to increase even though we were moving against the wind.

******

After a few minutes Harold and I both climbed up the mast for another look and Peter soon joined us. What we saw coming towards us on our starboard side was a vast array of cogs, galleys, and Arab dhows. Sails were everywhere.

"It's an entire fleet and a big one at that" ... "Those look like Algerian galleys, by God." ... "They be bound for Spain, probably Almeria or Malaga, if they hold their course."

"You're right, Harold, yes you are. It looks like the Moors are bringing an army over to Spain. Probably because of the fighting around Granada we heard about when we were in Lisbon."

I made up my mind quickly. It was too good of an opportunity to pass up.

"They won't be expecting us. So let's go see if there are any strays and stragglers we can take."

Prize money was always on everyone's mind; it was exactly the order Harold and his crew had been hoping to receive.

After we got closer to the Moorish fleet Harold and I climbed down the mast and hurried to the stern of the galley and bounded up the four wooden steps to the roof of the galley's stern castle. Peter stayed up on the mast to keep us informed.

Of course that's what we did. Every veteran archer knows the roof of a galley's stern castle is the best place from which to direct a fight at sea. They also know that lieutenants and senior sergeants don't climb masts and stay there unless there is something important to see.

Our men are all veterans; every one of them knew a fight was likely to be coming the moment Harold and I hurried across the deck and bounded up the stairs to the roof of the stern castle, particularly when we left Peter up on the mast with the lookouts and sent the passengers into the fore and stern castles to get them out of the way.

As I went up the steps the thought that crossed my mind was that we are the wolf that just found a large flock of sheep which might be guarded by dangerous dogs.

******

Less than an hour later we were well behind the Algerian fleet with a prey in sight and mind—a very big and very slow cog that was lumbering along and falling further and further behind the convoy. Unfortunately there was also an Algerian galley, a two decker like ours, about three thousand paces upwind of the cog, obviously the convoy's rear guard.

"Hoy the deck," came Peter's shout. "There are horses on the cog's deck; horses I say." *Well that got a murmur from the men, didn't it? If nothing else they'll have something to talk about for days.*

Harold and I looked at each other. "Horses?" We said to each other at the very same moment.

"Well," I said with a smile. "Henry and Raymond always said we needed more horses."

Harold just smiled grimly and nodded.

******

Taking the big Algerian cog turned out to have a big problem attached to it—the Algerian galley. We swept by the cog and the archers in our lookout nest quickly cleaned the cog of its lookout and several of its sailors who were foolish enough to show themselves.

From the roof of the stern castle Harold and I could see the rows of horses on the cog's deck. They were tied side by side to the deck railing on both sides of the deck. Peter shouted down that he thinks he may have caught a glimpse of more horses in the hold below the deck.

Our move towards the horse transport caused the Algerian galley to come surging forward to meet us. It was a two decker like ours as most galleys are, but slightly smaller and wider, and thus, so we reasonably assumed, slower than ours even in the unlikely event each of its oars was pulled by two able-bodied men with arms as strong as our archers' instead of the starving slaves usually used by the Moors.

Several frustrating hours later the Algerian convoy was long out of sight over the horizon and we were no closer to taking the horse cog than when we started. Our problem was quite basic—the horse cog might sail away and escape if we stopped to fight the galley; on the other hand, if we grappled the horse cog to board it we'd become an unmoving target and the Algerian galley would be able to ram us if its captain was so inclined.

At first, Harold kept us close to the horse cog and we tried to board it.

But each time we came alongside of the horse cog the Algerian galley closed in as if to ram us. So we would dance away and shower it with arrows until it backed off. Then we would row around to the far side of the cog and start again; whereupon the Algerian galley would come around the cog and once again come straight at us.

"Goddamnit, not again!" that was Harold's latest response when the Algerian came around the horse transport so we could see it once again from where we were standing.

We talked it over and finally came to a reluctant conclusion—our only hope is to concentrate on taking the Algerian galley as quickly as possible and then try to find the cog before it got too far away to be found.

Let's face it, the idea that we might be able to take a ship full of Arab horses was exciting and no one wanted to give it up, at least not me. Besides, here we are and the convoy is already well over the horizon and some distance away.

"Good. Let's do it. But Harold, do we have anyone on board who knows anything about horses?"

****** *William*

The captain of the Algerian galley seemed to understand our decision to change the way we were fighting—he left the horse cog and ran for it with the wind behind him. No doubt to draw us away from the cog. It was a smart thing to do and he succeeded.

We chased after the Algerian for the better part of an hour before we caught him. Once we did it was only a matter of time. Our massive flight of arrows cleared his deck and dropped into his rudder men and rowers until he stopped rowing and waited for us. The Algerian was wallowing in the oceans swells as we warily approached.

There was no resistance when we came along side and threw our grapples. Our prize crew and twenty additional archers poured over the deck railing and into the Algerian galley to secure its crew and free its slaves. In less than a minute the grapple lines were cast off and we swung around and began rowing hard for where Harold thought the horse cog might be found.

Samuel the tailor's apprentice from Newcastle and a long time archer was the galley's prize sergeant. Where Samuel heads from here will depend on the supplies and water he finds on board and the condition of the Algerian's slaves and crew. My guess is he'll probably head for Palma as it is the closest friendly port. From there he'll on to Malta, Crete, and Cyprus. We didn't stick around to find out.

The sun was just starting to go down and the strength of our rowers beginning to fade when our lookouts finally saw the sails of the horse cog plodding along in the distance. The fool captaining the cog had continued on his original course thinking that he was safe once we dropped out of sight over the horizon.

There was no resistance. As soon as we approached

the horse cog dropped its sails. There were no casualties on either side when we grappled the cog and our boarding party swarmed aboard.

Peter, Harold, and I went with the boarding party. So did a couple of former slaves among our sailors who claimed to be able to speak passable Arabic as Harold does from the years he spent as a Moorish slave after his London cog was taken.

What we found on the cog were forty one horses, a dozen or so sailors who are trembling and scared out of their minds thinking we are pirates who will kill them or sell them for slaves, and about twenty horse servants who are mostly young boys. All of the horse servants are Moors and, according to Harold, most and perhaps all of them are slaves with the possible exception of the white bearded older man who seems to be their sergeant.

Most of our men don't know much about horses other than how to harness them to ploughs and wagons. Almost all of us know how to do that, of course, being as most of us came from farming villages. Six or seven of Harold's archers, on the other hand, were former blacksmiths or hostlers including a couple of three stripe sergeants; and they were promptly summoned and added to the prize crew—and seemed quite pleased to be included.

Within minutes they were looking at the horses' teeth and hooves and consulting with each other and using the translators and Harold to talk to the white beard and the stable boys. On one thing they seem to be in total agreement—these are fine horses and they've been getting good care. Moors, they told each other knowingly, aren't mostly worth a damn as fighters but they certainly know their horses.

I myself know nothing about horses but these look very different from the plough horse I remember walking behind when I was a serf boy helping my ma throw seeds and plough for Sir Guy—they are beautiful and all sleek and shiny.

They look somewhat like the fast palfrey amblers used by our outriders and nothing at all like the big destriers used by Knights in tournaments or the strong and muscular coursers the gentry favour for campaigns. One of them particularly caught my eye despite my total ignorance of all things about horses—a sleek stallion the colour of a golden chestnut. Perhaps because it snorted and pawed the ground and shook its head as I walked past.

"That one, Harry" I told the Archer sergeant who was the prize's newly appointed sergeant captain as I stopped and looked. "I'd really like to have that one. Please try to get him to Cornwall for me."

Chapter Five
We take some prizes.

Our sailing plans were changed by taking the horses. There is no question but what we want to keep them. That meant there was also no question but that we must call in at Palma to take on water and food for the horses instead of continuing directly to Malta as we had once hoped.

Most of the archers and sailors on board are veterans and have been to the port of Palma on the island of Mallorca several times. Tori had not. This will be her first visit. Both the island and the city are rather small—so I suspect she's going to be very happy to set her feet on shore and very disappointed by its little market.

On the other hand, Palma is on Mallorca Island. It's an old walled city with an ancient port that was once a centre of the Islamic piracy that still flourishes in these waters. Today, however, the Moorish pirates are on the mainland in places such as Tunis and Algiers and Palma is truly a soft and quiet place under the nominal control of a batch of now-peaceful Moors from the people who call themselves "Berbers." They're such an ancient tribe that even they don't know what the name means, at least that what Harold says.

Maybe the Berbers of Mallorca were once the pirates but now they're apparently not, or so we were assured by the merchants the last time we put in here. The Algerian and Tunisian pirates from the other side of the water apparently swept the local boys from the Mediterranean years ago and left them to be farmers, fishermen, and merchants—and they're still a bit pissed about it.

The reason we're heading to Palma for water and supplies is that a few days ago Lisbon's merchants once again assured us that Mallorca's Berber king is still a deadly enemy of the Moslem Caliph who rules Tunis and Algiers—the man who is now in the process of sending reinforcements and horses to his army in Spain.

As I mentioned to Harold as we entered the harbour,

the tavern and the two ale houses in the mud next to the old stone quay weren't bad either, just smoky when it gets cold at night and their warming fires are lit. If I remember correctly, the tavern has great bread and goat cheese and an especially tart and tasty vinegar for dipping oiled bread and goat cheese into even though the girls smell bad and the wine is weak from too much water being added.

And that's how we found Palma when we reached it. All and all, if it hadn't changed since my last visit, Palma is a very nice place to make a port stop and replenish our stores even if the market is some distance from the quay. Genoa and Pisa have had commercial establishments here for years and there is even a little Catholic Church and a cemetery if one is into religion or needs burying.

Another good thing about Palma for Englishmen is that there appear to be few, if any, Venetians living here. I'm not sure why. Perhaps the other Italians who live here made it too difficult for them or they pissed off the local caliph by fighting with the other merchants the way they did in the Byzantine ports.

******

We rowed into Palma's ancient harbour towing the horse cog because the wind was unfavourable. What we didn't find was either Alan's or Gary's galleys; what we did find was our prize. The Algerian galley we had recently taken was anchored just off the city's old stone quay and taking on supplies from lighters.

That it had gotten to Palma before us was not a surprise—we'd stayed with the lumbering old horse cog and even towed it for a while yesterday when the winds failed. What was a surprise is that it was anchored in the harbour instead of being tied to the mooring posts on the quay.

Harold had suggested the prize galley come here and brought us to Palma to get water and stores because we'd heard it was still friendly and because we didn't have any problems when we'd made port calls here in the past. *Also we didn't have much choice because of the horses and their need for more food and water if we are to begin sending them on their way to Cornwall.*

As soon as we entered the harbour and saw the prize at anchor Harold, shouted an order across the water to the horse cog telling its prize captain to drop his anchor in the harbour and wait. Then we rowed to the prize galley instead of to the quay.

"We need to know why Steven anchored out here instead of at the quay," Harold explained with a nod towards the prize as the towing line was cast off and we temporarily parted ways with our new horses.

It was a false alarm. Harold and I climbed on to the prize as soon as our galley bumped up against it—and quickly learned there was no problem.

All was well. The new prize captain had anchored here out of an abundance of caution; he had freed the galley's slaves and doubled their rations as he'd been instructed but he was short of rowers and didn't want any of them to run until he got his new command safely to Cyprus.

Harold nodded his agreement, clapped its anxious prize sergeant, Samuel the one-time tailor on the shoulder, and told him he was doing a good job and to follow us and tie up at the quay. We promptly pushed off from the tailor's prize and proceeded back to the horse transport so we could finish towing it up to the city's quay.

The only surprise was the large number of sea gulls and pigeons that had begun circling the horse transport. The pigeons suddenly all swooped in and landed almost at the same time. The sea gulls soon followed them down.

****** *William*

Mooring at Palma was easy and fast. The quay was surprising quiet except for the birds that wheeled around the sky above us in hopes that we would drop something for them to swoop down and eat.

A couple of Arabs in ragged gowns grabbed the mooring lines as our sailors threw them, wrapped them around a couple of big rocks on the old stone quay, and then squatted down on their haunches to watch our arrival. It was a lovely warm day and the wind was light. Somewhere in the distance a dog was barking.

A strange looking cog with two masts was only one other transport at the quay. There was no activity around it so it was hard to tell whether it was loading or unloading or just marking time. Other than a couple of Arabs standing by to moor the approaching horse transport the Palma quay was empty—a far cry from the busy quays and wharves of London and Lisbon.

The tide was high so Tori and I were able to easily climb on to the quay as soon as the harbour workers grabbed the mooring lines our sailors threw to them and tied us up. It's not always so easy to get on and off a galley because most quays, including Palma's, were built primarily for use by cargo cogs whose decks sit much higher above the water. That's why galleys are sometimes pulled ashore on a nearby beach to be loaded and unloaded.

As we climbed over the galley's rail to get on to the quay I found myself wondering how far below the quay our galley would be sitting when we returned after the tide went out; and hoping that would be the least of our problems. Little did I know.

Tori and I walked with Harold and a couple of archers as guards down the cobblestoned waterfront street to the tiny little square stone building at the end of the quay which we knew to be the port captain's office. Tori waited outside with the archers whilst Harold and I entered.

It was a small stone building with two small window opening and a small door opening. The wooden door and the wooden shutters were open to light the interior.

We've been here before and the welcome was friendly as Harold and I walked through the door. Two elderly Arabs wearing turbans raised their hands and murmured some kind of ritual greeting as we ducked our heads to clear the doorway and enter. They were sitting on short three legged stools with their backs against the building's short stone wall.

We bowed and Harold began waving his arms towards the quay and chattering away in the Arabic he learned during his years as a Moorish galley slave. After a bit of chatter Harold nodded to the men in agreement, pulled a couple of coins from the coin purse tied to his belt, and handed them to one of the men with another little bow.

That fetched a satisfied nod and a couple of toothless smiles in return.

Then we went off to see the local merchants who provide water and supplies to visiting shipping. We didn't have to go far. They were already gathering in front of the doorway as we came out of the port office.

Once again there were the traditional greetings and then quite a bit of chatter and negotiations.

"It took longer than usual because of the hay and corn for the horses," Harold explained after the ritual bows and hand slappings when the negotiations were completed. Then we began walking on the muddy footpath towards the city gate to go to the market.

******

We spent the afternoon walking through the city's somewhat deserted market. Tori was disappointed because there wasn't much to see except the usual foods and supplies for the local residents. It was just as well, the lack of people in the market I mean, because the merchants weren't busy and had time to talk.

Most of the merchants were Moslems and Jews but there were also several Genoans and Pisans among them. We'd done business with them on previous visits and were greeted as if we were long lost relatives who had finally returned.

The merchants inevitably offered us tea and were quite friendly. If anything, they went out of their way to make it quite clear how pleased they are that we'd taken the Algerian shipping and horses. They seemed to know all the details.

News of our prizes obviously spread quickly among the market's merchants. That's not surprising since the market was almost empty of potential customers and prior to our arrival they had been mostly standing around in little groups talking.

The only excitement came when a breathless sergeant from Harold's galley came running up to interrupt us with a report that Alan's and Gary's galleys had just come into the harbour together with a Moorish prize loaded with amphorae containing olive oil and corn. Somehow that seemed important so we hurried back to the quay to learn more about it. It also must have been of interest to the merchant who overheard the report; as we left I could see him hurrying off to spread the news.

Later that day we came back for another visit to the market. It was much busier and we received lots of inquisitive looks from the eyes of the Moslem women hidden behind their face masks.

The relative handful of Genoan and Pisan merchants in the city are an altogether another matter. They're like the island's Jewish and Moslem merchants—all smiles and happy enough to sell us supplies and take our coins in the market place and pay us to carry their cargos and money orders.

On the other hand, according to the other merchants in the market the Genoans and Pisans are not at all happy to see us in Palma once again. We may not be their mortal enemies, the Venetians, but they know about our concessions and trading posts and money order parchments elsewhere in the Mediterranean and about our war galleys and ferocious archers—they fear we'll come here next and set up to be their competitors.

What the Latin merchants don't know, of course, is that they needn't worry for a while; we're still a long way off from being ready to set up a post here on the island. We have other more important bread to bake in places like Lisbon, Piraeus, and Malta.

On the other hand, of course, they're right to be concerned because someday, sooner or later, we'll undoubtedly set up a post here if our affairs continue to grow and prosper.

Unfortunately that day is still a long way off because ports such as Lisbon and Piraeus have so much more potential—so we'll do as we've always done when we're here and go all out to convince everyone that we are friendly and just passing through on our way to the Holy Land.

Of course we're acting friendly and peaceful. I've said it before and I'll say it again—it isn't good to shite where you walk and we almost certainly will want to stop here again as we come and go between Cornwall and Cyprus.

I also don't trust the local ruler, if only because he's a Moslem. It's well known that they'll change sides in an instant and cut off your head if one of their priests tells them that's what God wants or they start listening to their women. They're like our Christian kings and Popes in that.

******

My lieutenants and Tori and I ate and drank wine in the courtyard of a tavern near the quay that evening. All the sergeants were invited and we had quite a good time including moors dancing that somehow got started—which turned out to be great good fun and very bad dancing because none of us had danced together before and everyone knew different steps and moves.

It was an evening with much laughing and good natured pointing and jibes, particularly when the sergeants got the tavern girls to join the dancing and everyone kept bumping into each other and trying to do different things at the same time.

And it wasn't just an evening of drinking and play.

My three lieutenants and I sat together with Tori at the end of one of the tables. In between the eating and drinking and moors dancing we decided how we would get the horses safely back to Cornwall, what to do with the oil and corn in the new prize, and how the galleys and cogs will be crewed with the available archers and the newly freed slaves.

The big decision was that Gary's galley is to escort the horse cog as far as Lisbon with forty of our veteran archers and a good sergeant on board in case they get separated from Gary's galley and run into pirates.

There are very few pirates after Lisbon so the horse cog will go on alone from Lisbon with just its prize crew and a dozen archers under a three stripe sergeant; Gary will board the rest of the archers and come back here to replenish his supplies and follow us on to Constantinople.

Most of the pirates are out here between Cyprus and Gibraltar these days; we've pretty much cleaned them out between Cyprus and the Holy Land ports.

Some of us linked arms and sang and danced as we staggered back to our galleys; others stayed with the tavern girls to dip their dingles. I gave the smiling tavern keeper a gold bezant to pay for everyone's food and drink. It was well worth it.

The dingle dippers were on their own.

Chapter Six

I fight for my life.

Everything seemed normal the next day when Tori and I and a small escort of archers set off for the market for another day of shopping ashore.

I was talking to a Jewish merchant about tunics when all of a sudden there was a great commotion and the market stalls around us began to be hurriedly closed. Someone shouted something to our merchant and his face blanched.

"You must run. Go to your galleys. Hurry. Hurry." he shouted over his shoulder as he turned and dashed to the back of his stall and out the narrow back doorway that revealed itself when he pushed aside a dirty linen curtain.

It was too late. Several dozen armed men came surging around the corner and into the market—and came straight at us. And so did two men who had been loitering nearby.

I leaned across a small table covered with linens and pulled an astonished Tori right off her feet—and threw her behind me with my left hand whilst I tried to draw my sword with my right. Too late. I felt a tremendous punch in the ribs as I started to draw my sword.

My assailant was a tall lean man with a heavy black beard and incredible bad breath. His knife stuck in my chain for a second—then he instinctively raised it and sliced it across my arm, neck, and cheek as I punched him in the face with the handle of my sword as I brought it out and swung it towards the second man.

The second man was running at me so hard with a knife in his hand that the bloody point of my sword came out his back as he ran onto it—and pulled it right out of my hand as he screamed and twisted away. His knife missed me before he dropped it as he twisted away and went down grabbing at the blade of my sword with both hands.

"Harry, throw me your shield and run for the galleys. Fetch reinforcements. Hurry man. Hurry."

That's what I shouted as I motioned towards the disappearing merchant and desperately shouted my order to the archer who happened to be standing nearest to the back of the shop.

I picked up the shield he threw at me as he turned around to run and reached over to pull my sword out of the now-gasping assassin who now had a stream of blood pouring out of his mouth and was still holding on to the blade of my sword with both hands.

I was trying to pull my sword out of the assassin's chest and he was still gasping and holding it and trying to scream when the first of the surging and shouting mob reached us.

My four remaining archers had their swords out and

their galley shields up as I reached to retrieve my sword. What was good is that one of the archers had picked up Tori when I literally pulled her off her feet and threw her behind me and stepped in front of her with his sword and shield up and ready; what was bad was that we were seriously outnumbered.

I used my borrowed shield to block the sword of the first man who reached me just as I finished pulling my own sword out of the assassin—and swept it across the man's face. He screamed and fell off to the side holding his face with both hands and I semi-staggered backward into the little line of archers that had instinctively formed up at the back of the shop in front of Tori.

I knew I was bleeding from a head wound because I could see the drops of blood fly as I moved about. But at least it wasn't getting in my eyes.

Our attackers pushed into the little stall to get at us. That gave us an advantage as the men in the front were being pushed forward and off balance by those in the rear behind them. There was much clanging and thudding and a terrible din because we were all screaming and shouting.

A big overweight man in an Arab gown stumbled over the man whose face I slashed and would have fallen on against me—except I speared him with sword straight into his eye whilst I held him and his sword away from me with my shield. Even so he backed me up a couple of paces.

It was the same on both sides of me. The weight of our close-packed attackers was pressing us backwards as those in the rear pushed and tried to climb over those going down in front of us. Slowly but surely we were being pushed out of the narrow back door of the shop and into the little alley behind it.

The doorway out of the rear of the shop was narrow. That gave me hope as one by one we were pressed through it. I was the third man who backed through the doorway. Now only a short tough-looking archer with the broad shoulders of a strong bowman was holding the door. The other archer in the guard must have gone down inside the shop.

I darted a quick look down the alley. So far it's empty except for the four of us and Tori. That's good. But we have to hold the doorway. If they press us back into the alley they'll be able to come at us from all sides at once and it will be all over.

It took a while and happened quickly even though it seemed to me that it occurred very slowly—two blades stabbed at the broad shouldered archer in the doorway at the same time, one high and one low. I screamed a warning but there was nothing the archer could do. He turned away one of the blades with his shield; the other went straight into his throat and pushed him out of the doorway.

Before anyone else could get through the little doorway I chopped down on the arm pushing the sword into the archer's throat so hard I could feel my blade bite all the way through the wrist holding the sword. I never did see the face of the man whose hand I chopped off for he jerked the stump back—and that gave me a chance to step sideways into the doorway to take the dying archer's place.

What I saw was a little room not much bigger than a couple of horse stalls filled with a disorganized and packed mass of shouting and screaming men climbing and tripping over the bodies of those who were already down—some to get at me and some who were wounded obviously trying to stagger and crawl away.

Everything was chaos and confusion. I don't know how long I held the doorway, or how many men I fought, but there were at least several including one I pushed back with my shield and barely pinked with about three inches of iron into his heart as he was falling backwards over someone already on the floor.

Then I watched a blade slip under my raised shield and take me in the thick of my leg above my knee and go all the way through and come out the back. It was a cold comfort that it got me at the same moment I slashed someone else's neck so hard that his head almost came off.

It was strange—I could see the sword go all the way through my leg and out the back but at first I couldn't feel it.

I reeled backwards in a desperate and instinctive effort to get off the blade. That's when I realised that the other two archers in the alley were on either side of me at the alley door—when they both simultaneously stabbed their swords deep into the body of the man who was leaning forward to push his sword further into my leg so I could not get off it.

His eyes widened in surprise and the look on his face turned from ferocious satisfaction to dismay as he realised he was dead and let go of his sword with a scream.

"Go down the alley and look for a place to hide" I gasped as I turned back to a white faced Tori standing aghast against the far wall of the narrow alley. She didn't do as I said. Instead she ran towards me and the sword sticking almost all the way through the upper part of my leg.

****** *Geoffrey the monger's son*

I was carving a piece of wood and yarning with my mates Alfie and Georgie in the shade of the stern castle when I heard Robert Farmer's unbelievable call from the mast. Poor old Robert was on duty up in the lookout's nest for his sins whilst the rest of us were waiting to be released for a few hours of shore leave. I'm overdue for a drink and tavern girl and so are Alfie and Georgie, and that's for damn sure.

"Alert on deck. Alert I say. Danger on the quay. Sound the alarm. Sound the alarm. Alert I say, alert."

We all sprang to our feet and looked about wildly. Then we ran for our weapons as Lieutenant Peter ran across the deck and jumped on castle roof for a quick look about.

"Blow the alert horn; blow repel boarders." The Lieutenant suddenly shouted. "Blow it, goddamn you; hurry man hurry. Repel boarders, no drill. No drill."

Over and over again Jacob the horn man began blowing two long toots and three short ones.

"Repel boarders, no drill; repel boarders, no drill." The sergeants began screaming as they repeated the lieutenant's order.

The deck was all confusion as we ran for our swords and pikes and everyone tried to get a shield off the racks at the same time. I was just pulling a shield off its peg when I happen to look down the quay and saw one of our men running and staggering along towards us holding his sword and waving and shouting.

Alert horns and drums began sounding on our other galleys moored along the quay at about the same time. *What the hell is going on here.*

Lieutenant Peter screamed "follow me" as he vaulted up on to the deck rail and climbed on to the quay waving his sword. So me and the boys poured off the galley and followed him. Of course we did.

The lieutenant stopped by the staggering man for an instant. Then, as the man fell on to his hands and knees, the lieutenant waved his sword at me and the men coming off the galley, shouted "follow me, archers, follow me," and began running like a madman for the city gate.

I can runner, better than most I think, but it was all I could do to keep up with the lieutenant. Several men passed me even though I'm a good runner, I really am; I used to win the Sunday races after church, didn't I?

We pounded up the path and through the gate on the cobblestones and ran towards the city's market. I was near the front and could see a long line of archers running hard behind me. Most of the shops we passed were closed and empty although some had people cowering in the back. It wasn't until we came around a corner that we suddenly heard the noise and shouts of a battle and saw men on the ground and staggering away from the front of a large merchant's stall.

I saw how many men were jammed into the merchant's

stall as I charged towards it behind Lieutenant Peter and the thrusters who had run past me. It was absolutely packed with Arab men so close together they was that some of them couldn't even get their weapons up; and, best of all, they were mostly looking away from us and trying to get to the fighting in the rear of the stall.

Them looking in the wrong direction was a bad mistake, and that's for sure. The lieutenant reached them first began chopping them down and so did the rest of us a few seconds later.

"Rescue. Rescue. Kill. Kill." that's what Lieutenant Peter kept shouting and we all took up the call.

A pike man named James from the lower rowing deck was next to me as I ran into the shop. We immediately formed a bit of a team when James promptly stabbed an Arab in the back and I just as promptly chopped him in the side of his neck when he sort of turned around with a look of surprise on his face. As you might imagine, the Arab dropped the sword he'd been holding in the air over his head and went down with a scream.

James and I made a good combination—he stabbed and jabbed at everyone he could reach, usually in the back or as they tried to turn around, and I moved along the side of his pike and slashed at their necks and faces as they tried to turn around—then they'd go down and we'd walk over them and those already on the ground to get at the next Arab. *It wasn't that easy, of course, but you get the idea.*

There were already a lot of men on the ground as we entered so we mostly were walking and standing on bodies as fought our way in. And that wasn't as easy as it sounds, let me tell you, because we were all slipping and sliding as we climbed on and over the pile of men who were already down, particularly since a good number of them were still moving and trying to get up.

As we got closer to the back of the merchant's stall I could see one of our men in the rear doorway fighting off the Arabs. He was wounded but using his shield and sword with deadly effect on the Arabs trying to reach him.

A few seconds later I climbed over the pile of bodies, cut my way all the way through to the doorway, and jumped out into the alley behind it. James burst out right behind me and then Lieutenant Peter and more and more of our men came through. There were dead and wounded archers in the alley including Captain William all bloody. His woman was there too. She was trying to pull a sword out of his leg.

Then the screams and cries and chopping sounds from inside the store began to quiet down and I could hear Lieutenant Peter, and then the sergeants, begin shouting "take prisoners; take prisoners."

******

Tori reached me as I stood in the alley with half of the dead Arab's sword sticking out the back of my leg.

"Go now. Run Tori. You must. Hurry damn you."

"No. No." She screamed as she grabbed my arm to help hold me up. "I can't. I won't."

"Then pull it out. Hurry pull it out. Grab the handle and pull. That's it; pull." *It's got to come out; I can't fight with this thing sticking in me like this.*

She tried and that's the last thing I remember before I apparently sat down against the alley wall and went to sleep for a few minutes.

I was still holding my sword when I woke up to a lot of noise and shouting and screaming coming from inside the shop. One of the archers who had taken my place at the door was sitting against the wall unmoving with his eyes staring out into space. The other archer who had taken my place was still at the door.

Suddenly the archer at the door stepped aside and a wild eyed two striper jumped from on top of the stack of bodies in front of the door and into the alley with a bloody sword in one hand and a ship's shield in the other. Another archer carrying a bloody pike burst through the doorway right behind him.

Moments later Tori was trying to help me stand up and we watched as Peter and more and more archers came pouring out of the door and into the alley. Then I must have gone back to sleep for a moment.

I vaguely remember, at least I think I remember, waking up and being bounced along and a lot of people talking who sounded out of breath. My face and shield arm felt like they were on fire but then the fire went away and I somehow felt very safe.

"Careful there. All right, lift him up. Easy goddamnit. Easy." *Oh good. Harold and Peter are here. Things will be better now.*

"Tell me what happened," I gasped as I suddenly woke up and felt and saw Tori trying to wash my face with some kind of rag. Before anyone could answer I felt a terrible pain as a sailor began using a sail sewing needle to sew up the slashes in my arm and the side of my neck and face. That's when I went back to sleep.

Chapter Seven

Life goes on.

Suddenly I realised I ached all over and was face-up on a ship's deck with a circle of familiar faces looking down at me anxiously—Harold, Peter, Tori and many others.

"What happened?" I asked as Tori knelt and lifted my head to put a pinch of flower paste in my cheek to kill the pain and give me a sip from a bowl of ale. It was so good.

"You got yourself sliced up a bit and there's no half way about it," Peter answered from somewhere. "But we've got you back on board and all nicely sewed up. You'll be back on your feet and moors dancing in no time."

"Why? Who did it? Here, help me up."

"No," Peter and Tori both answered simultaneously.

Peter was emphatic that I not try to get up with Harold standing next to him nodding his total agreement.

"You can get up soon but not yet," Peter said. "You best stay down until you're more steady on your feet and we're sure you've stopped bleeding."

"As to who did it? We're don't know yet—but we took five of their wounded alive so we'll find out for sure before we finish them off." Peter said it with a grim tone of certainty to his voice. He had a bandage on his arm and blood splattered all over his tunic.

I could see Peter start to say something more and Harold was opening his mouth to speak when the lookout on the mast suddenly shouted important news in some barely understandable village version of English.

"Hoy izz deck. Look youz. People be comz out yon gate. They'uns izz belooks gentry."

What I remember most when I heard the lookout's call was that Tori was gently stroking my face and the other side of my face and neck felt as if they were on fire. I didn't know at the time that my clothes had been cut off and I was laying in the sun on a galley's gently rocking deck completely naked.

The realization that I was laid out completely naked on a galley deck didn't register with me until a few minutes later when something I heard came to me when I was resting with my eyes closed—and caused me to open them and search around my stomach and waist with my hand to see if it was true. It came when I heard Peter turn down someone's request with an angry tone to his voice.

"No. They cannot talk to the captain; he's too sick and not dressed proper. Tell them to wait there. I'll talk to them."

******

It wasn't until the next morning that I got more of the story. I woke up on the wooden deck when the galley lurched from a little wave and the sun shined in my eyes when I opened them.

Tori and a couple of archers were sitting with me and I

was terribly thirsty and hungry and ached with a throbbing pain in my leg and a burning sensation on my arm and the side of my face. There was some kind of clothe draped over me.

"Good; you're awake. How do you feel?" was Tori's anxious inquiry as she reached out to hold my hand.

"Thirsty and hungry," I croaked weakly. *My God, is that my voice?*

One of the archers jumped to his feet and returned almost immediately with a bowl of breakfast ale and a piece of flatbread so fresh and warm that he must have snatched it straight off the fire.

Tori was still ripping off little chunks of bread and dipping them in ale to feed me when Peter came rushing up. He too asked me how I felt—and then Harold came and asked also. After a while they told me what they knew about the attack.

"The Caliph himself came down to the quay to see you and apologize on behalf of the city. He said he would take the head of every man involved and levy a special tax on the market to fully pay for all the damages and all the trouble. Even better, he has granted us a trading concession, the right to have a defensible post, and use of the quay with no fees or taxes."

"Well that's something of a surprise."

"Not really," said Harold with a grin. "According to the merchants who came to see us after he left, the Caliph is like everyone else—he's scared shitless. He's heard all kinds of stories about you and your fearsome English archers and galleys. The fact we killed most of the toughs who attacked you and drowned the ones we questioned merely convinced him even more."

"And the Caliph's right, you know, Captain. If they had killed you or Tori we surely would have sacked the city and hung his head on the city gate. As it was, it was all I could do to keep the men from sacking the city. They're madder than hell. They wanted to burn the place down, didn't they?"

"So who did it and why?" I croaked, and then had to motion with a little wave of my hand for Tori to give me another sip of ale.

"Well, that's what's so interesting, isn't it?" said Peter.

"According to the merchants, all the attackers were part of a company of local villains who were selling protection to the local people and merchants. Those we caught all said the same thing before we tossed them in the harbour. So it's probably true."

"Do you believe them?" I asked.

"Yes, I think I do. We weren't gentle with the men we caught. They were anxious to tell us everything they knew before we threw them over the side to drown. I'm sure they would have told us if they'd known who paid for the attack—and so is everyone who listened to them sob and scream their stories."

******

I was stiff and sore but able to ride out to the cemetery on the back of a horse cart with Tori to help one of the local priests say the words when we buried our three dead archers. We put them in the local cemetery where

Christians and other non-Moslems are buried—then we went back to our galleys and all but one of them immediately set sail for Lisbon or Malta.

We left Alan and his galley behind to gather any additional information that might become available about our attackers. He'll wait a few days to get any news that might come in and then follow us to Malta.

Our problem is simple—we still don't know why the attack occurred and who was responsible or why they did it—and perhaps we never will since it appears the head of the city's protection gang was not among the dead and cannot be found.

In any event, there is, so it is claimed, a big reward for information and both the merchants and the caliph's men are trying to find out who paid for the attack and, at least so they also claim, searching for any of the attackers who might have escaped. Maybe we'll know more when and if any of them are caught.

"Peter, did you ask the merchants or the Caliph's men if there are any Venetians in the city?"

******

I was still stiff and sore and swollen but able to stand and walk slowly about the galley deck by the time we reached Malta. I've been here so often and like it so much that it was almost like coming home when we rowed into the harbour. We came in alone; somehow we'd lost touch with Gary's galley and the prize a couple of nights ago even though the night skies had been relatively clear.

Brindisi himself came galloping down to the quay on a

horse as we were mooring. He said he knew we were coming and had been waiting for us—and promptly led Tori and me and Peter to his favourite tavern in the city for a bowl of wine "and what I miss most these days—lots of good conversation about what's going on in the outside world."

We talked as we walked and it took a while to get there because I am still limping badly and walking slowly. Brindisi took one of my arms and Tori the other and we made it with Peter and a couple of archers leading the way. I was tired and happy to be able to sit down and catch my breath when we finally got there.

The tavern stood by itself down the muddy lane off the city's old quay. It must be Brindisi's favourite for it was the very same place where I'd first met the flamboyant old pirate those many years ago. We'd gone there for something to eat and Brindisi had been there to have his fortune told. That was back when he was a newly retired pirate and recently ennobled and his hair was grey instead of the white it is today.

"I heard about Palma and the Venetians having a go at you in the market. You look like shite, by the way. Are you alright? Tell me about it."

"Venetians? Who told you they were Venetians?" was my response. *And how do you know so much so soon?*

"Well it wasn't the Moors according to my spies over there on the other side of the water; so it must have been the Venetians. Who else hates you so much?"

Brindisi said it grandly with a smile at Tori and a rounding sweep of his bowl in the air to signal the tavern girl for another round even though we'd barely started on the first.

We talked about various things for a while. Then the jovial old pirate leaned forward with a conspiratorial air and surprised me.

"Sicily is weak these days and I'm getting old and have no heir. What would you think if I sold this place to the Templars? That's what Richard did with Cyprus, don't you know?"

******

We left for Piraeus two days later with much to think about. Brindisi asked me to do something I already intended to do—set up a post here. What truly surprised me was that he asked me station a substantial force of the archers and galleys here and take over his fortress so he can retire to a house he is building on the other side of the island.

Harold and Peter and I talked about Malta and the things we'd heard about it every day as we sailed and rowed towards Greece. They were positive and excited about the prospect of having a major base there instead of a small post as we'd initially planned.

I'm still not sure about Malta. Perhaps my lack of enthusiasm about taking on new responsibilities was because I still hurt and still have trouble walking; perhaps I'm just getting old. I wish Thomas and Yoram were here to talk about things.

"It's the perfect location for a major base on the trade routes to the Greek ports and to the Holy Land. That's why we always stop there, isn't it?" asked Harold. He was all for having a big post on Malta, Harold was; he wanted another port for his galley and cogs in case the Saracens take the Holy Land ports and we end up losing Cyprus or not needing it so much.

We talked about Malta and what happened at Palma and argued and planned all the way to Piraeus. That's the main port of the Greek capitol of Athens and another place where we've already decided to establish a trading post.

A fortified trading post on Malta is one thing; permanently stationing a strong force of archers and transports there and effectively taking over control of the island is another. Would the king in Sicily agree? What would he and Brindisi expect from us?

******

Circling seagulls and the stench of rotten fish filled the air as we rowed into Piraeus's great harbour. It was filled with all kinds of shipping from little fishing boats to huge cargo cogs and strange looking Moorish ships from the other side of the great desert.

Apparently we just missed a large Venetian convoy sailing to carry supplies and reinforcements to the crusaders at Constantinople. According to the port fee collector and the merchants, the Venetian fleet left the harbour this very morning a few hours before we arrived.

You might think it strange that the Venetians would stop here in Athens' great port of Piraeus whilst en route to fight the Greeks at Constantinople. I certainly was. But it seems the local merchants and the city's governor were quite pleased about the visit of the Venetian galleys and transports—both for the coins they received and because they are going to Constantinople.

Truth be told, they all confided to us in various ways, Athens will be more important and the Orthodox Church will be headquartered here if Constantinople falls to the crusaders.

"If it happens that Constantinople falls," a portly merchant cheerfully assured me whilst we were negotiating for the sale of the cargo of oil and corn on the prize cog, "it will be the will of God and I'll sell more corn."

******

"Lights ahead. Many lights," came the cry from the lookout in the masthead nest in the middle of the night.

I must have been awake in my bed because I heard it quite clearly. So I carefully pushed back the covers of my bedding so as to not disturb Tori or rip my stitches and stood up. I ducked my head to get out to the deck through the low doorway in forward castle went out on the galley's deck.

Nothing was to be seen so I walked back past the mast and carefully climbed up on the roof of the stern castle for a better look. As I slowly climbed stairs one stair at a time I heard the stern castle's door bang open and, a few seconds later, Harold climbed the stairs in two fast steps and stood next to me on the roof. I could make him out quite clearly even though we only had the light of a quarter moon.

At first we couldn't see the lights the lookout reported. They were still too low over the horizon. But then the galley rose on an ocean swell I saw a light ahead of us and, moments later, another and then many.

"We've caught up with the Venetian convoy carrying supplies and reinforcements to the crusaders at Constantinople," Harold said.

"There certainly are a lot of them," I offered.

"Aye Captain, that be true, yes indeedy," was Harold's response. "And they're sailing in the same direction towards Constantinople as we be sailing. It's almost certainly the Venetian convoy. But there's no sense taking chances and find ourselves in a fleet of Moorish pirates; I'm going to hold back here behind them until the sun comes up and we know for sure."

Then with a smile in his voice Harold added the real reason he wanted to hold back.

"Besides if we stay back here behind them we might come across a pirate what's come out to pick up the convoy's stragglers. The boys wouldn't mind getting some prize money for the taking of a pirate, no they wouldn't; neither would I for that matter."

"Aye, you're right Harold; yes you are, my friend. And more's the pity that we aren't sure it was the Venetians who ordered the attack in Palma—there are likely a lot of fat merchantmen in front of us we'd want to be taking if we knew for sure it was the Venetians."

******

Morning dawned with a huge convoy of Venetian transports in front of us and not a pirate to be seen. Disappointment showed on every face.

"By God, I've an idea," I said with a chuckle as I broke my nightly fast by munching some warm bread and drinking a bowl of morning ale.

"Let's have some moors dancing to cheer the men up and row right through the bastards at our fastest spissd so they can watch us dance as we go past."

And that's what we did as soon as the men finished eating their morning bread and cheese. Moreover, Harold announced a very big prize—whichever team of dancers wins will get the first shore leave when we reach Constantinople.

We were moving right along as we reached the rear of the Venetian fleet. We had a fairly good idea where the fleet captain was located because his ship had been flying three blue lights and all the others only a single white light—he's on a big cog at the front of the convoy.

Our drums were beating, our horn blower tootling, the men chanting, and the Moors dancers dancing as we dashed straight through the mass of Venetian shipping bringing supplies and more crusaders to Constantinople. It was if we were moving and they were standing still. Harold and Peter and Tori and I stood on the stern castle roof to watch the dancers and judge their dancing.

Everywhere the Venetian sailors and their crusader passengers rushed to their deck railings and watched as we came flying past with our dancers dancing on the deck. They inevitably waved and shouted we waved and shouted back most cheerfully.

The fleet captain's cog was no different. It's railing was crowded as we came past so close that our oars almost touched its hull.

I stood on the stern castle roof with a big smile and

made a great circular winding motion with my arm as we dashed past. We had the wind behind us and two strong men at every oar.

"I don't think there's a ship in the world that could catch us and certainly none of that lot."

Harold said it with a great deal of satisfaction in his voice as he gestured toward the Venetians we were rapidly leaving behind.

The sailors were once again the clear winners of the dance contest. The galley's sailors all lustily cheered when their team's victory was announced, even those who hadn't danced. So did the archers in the second and third place teams when Harold stood on the stern castle's roof and said it was too close to call so they could join the sailors in the first four-hour liberty party.

Chapter Eight
William

We rowed past the usual thousands and thousands of fishermen lining the shore and reached our quay at Constantinople about three hours after sunrise. Four of our galleys were moored at our quay and the area between our quay and the walls was filled with hundreds of refugees, a number of archers engaged in their required daily archery practise, and a couple of luckless men marching punishment drills. A great haze of dirty brown smoke hung over the city.

Henry recognized Harold's galley and trotted up with the senior sergeant in charge of our Constantinople post as soon as we arrived. Henry's jaw dropped and his eyes opened wide with concern and anger as soon as he saw my face. He instantly jumped down on to the deck and grabbed me by both shoulders in a gentle hug before I could even start to climb off.

I know how I look. I made Tori give me the mirror she had hidden and looked at myself. I look like shite even though Tori washed my face and trimmed my beard a couple of days ago. The stitches and slashes on my face and neck make me look hideous.

"My God. What the hell happened? Who did it?"

Once again the story came tumbling out. Harold and Peter and Tori stood on the deck next to me and told most of it. I mostly just stood there and listened with a few nods and shrugs and contributed a few minor corrections.

Henry was beside himself with anger and indignation. He was quite emotional and it touched me.

"Those fucking Venetians. It's got to have been them. There's rumours in the city that a huge Venetian fleet is on its way with supplies and reinforcements for the crusaders. They're starving across the way, aren't they? It serves the bastards right."

"Well the Greeks are right about the Venetians coming with supplies and more crusaders," said Harold. "We sailed right through the Venetian fleet three days ago. They'll be here in a day or two depending on the wind."

Then Harold got Henry to smile by telling him how we'd danced our way through the Venetian fleet and I'd gestured at the fleet's captain as we went dashing past his cog.

******

An hour later I was sitting a stool in the shade of the city wall as a hastily summoned pair of Greek healers careful looked at all my stitches and my leg. A good job of stitching the older one finally announced through an interpreter and no sign of the rotting pox even though my arm and my face and my leg are still red and swollen. *The Greeks may be corrupt and undependable but for some reason everyone thinks all the best healers and barbers are Greeks. I wonder why that is.*

I had to laugh when Harold made the mistake of asking the healers if they intended to bleed me. The older Greek got absolutely irate and rounded on him. His eyes flashed and he ranted and raved in Greek and shouted and shook his finger in Harold's face for at least a minute. The final wave of his hand and snort of disdain was clearly dismissive as he turned and gestured for me to stand up and follow him and for one of his assistants to fetch the stool.

Our translator's version of the long Greek tirade was short and to the point. "The healer says bleeding wounded men makes them worse." *I immediately resolved to ask the translator what the healer really said when Harold isn't around.*

The Greek made me follow him out into the sun and take off my Egyptian gown and codpiece all the way off. He put his head close to mine and looked at my eyes and teeth and even grabbed my tongue and pulled it way out and smelled it. Then he sat me back on the stool and proceeded to cut my stitches with a little knife and pluck out my stitches one at a time with his fingernails and smell them before he threw them on the ground. A great circle of very serious archers stood silently around me and watched intently.

Cutting the threads and pulling them out seemed to go on forever and it hurt like hell. Worse, goddamnit, I couldn't yelp and tried not to wince because the archers were watching. Harold and Henry said the men are furious and talking of revenge. They are convinced it was the Venetians and they are taking the attack personally.

When the healer finally finished sniffing the last thread he said something to one of his assistants and motioned for me to stay seated. The translator repeated what he said.

"He says the smell is good and you must show your wounds to the sun for one hour three times each day for seven days. He'll come back tomorrow. His assistant will stay with you until he returns. Also you should say prayers twice each day and not eat chicken livers until the weather gets colder."

"Harold, please make sure the healers look at the rest of our wounded and thoroughly dose them before they go."

******

The galleys and cogs of the Venetian relief fleet began appearing two days after Tori and I reached Constantinople. We watched from the quay as they anchored just off from crusader camp across the waterway and began using their small boats to bring the new supplies and crusaders ashore. The result on this side of the water is a city humming with rumours and fears of an imminent attack by the greatly strengthened crusaders.

I was feeling better and better and limping less every day. By the time the Venetian fleet finished unloading I'd made up my mind about what to do next. There is almost certainly going to be more fighting and more refugee hauling opportunities—so before it starts I need to make contact with the crusaders and negotiate a contract similar to the one we had at Zara.

Harold and Henry and Peter were in agreement with the idea that we need to make an agreement with the crusaders and appalled and opposed as to how I intended to go about getting it—by going across to the crusader camp on Harold's galley and walking into their camp alone.

And that's what I did as soon as the Venetian transports finished unloading the crusaders' supplies and reinforcements.

We just rowed in as if we owned the place and dropped our anchor in the midst of the Venetian fleet anchored just off the crusader camp.

The galley I came on was captained by Harold. He's got six stripes as the lieutenant commanding all of our company's galleys. It's Harold's personal command and it's a beauty—eighty eight oars and long and narrow. She's built for speed and is one of the fastest galleys afloat even when the deck is crowded with the usual sheep and cattle and the firewood we need to cook them and bake our bread on long voyages.

What was quite astonishing to everyone except Harold

and our veterans was that we weren't challenged as we rowed in and anchored in the middle of the Venetian cogs anchored just off the crusader camp—and close to the Venetian galleys which had been partially pulled ashore a little further down the beach.

No one paid us a bit of attention—probably because we were flying a Venetian flag and acted as if we belonged.

It probably also helped that the one change we'd made besides flying a Venetian flag was to have everyone on the deck except me take off their light brown Egyptian smocks with their front and back rank stripes.

Tori was furious and worried and my lieutenants, Harold, Henry, and Peter, didn't much like it that I was going ashore alone, but I insisted. Only one thing really bothered me besides my sore leg—climbing down into the galley's little dinghy wearing my chain mail. It and my two wrist knives are concealed under my Egyptian gown with its seven captain's stripes sewn on its front and back.

I always wear my two wrist knives but I almost didn't wear the chain. I know how to swim but I' not very good at it. There's no doubt about it, I'll sink like a stone if I ever go into deep water wearing it.

A couple of Harold's older two stripe sailors rowed me ashore. They'll wait until either I return or they are threatened and forced to leave. If they are forced to leave they'll hold a little off shore and be prepared to dart in and pick me up.

Both of my rowers are dependable Englishmen and very experienced boatmen. I made sure of that in case I needed to give them a message to carry back to Harold and

Peter. They nodded, mumbled their agreement and understanding, and rowed briskly when I pointed to where I wanted them to put me ashore and wait for my return.

As usual, the water off Constantinople was not at all rough the way it often is along the English coast. I'll have to ask Thomas why that is. What is even more surprising is that somehow it isn't the same colour either.

But the water was interesting and full of life—the sun was such whilst the sailors were rowing me to the shore that I could see the shadows of numerous fish darting here and there just below the surface. Most were fairly small but every so often I caught sight of a big one.

That's one thing I've noticed every time I've been here, the fish I mean. They probably explain all the little fishing boats and the people fishing shoulder to shoulder along the shore in front of the city walls across the way.

It's actually quite significant, all the fish and fishermen. It means starving Constantinople into submission would probably be close to impossible since the city walls come almost right up the water on three sides of the city—because the fishermen who are lined up shoulder to shoulder every day, and also those who are near the shore in their small boats, are always under the direct protection of defenders on the walls above them.

My two sailors nosed the dinghy into a gravelly beach right in front of the tents of the crusader camp. There are even more tents and shelters and people standing about than last time I saw the camp earlier this year; they're thick on the ground all the way up and over the top of the little hill that runs up from the beach.

Some of the tents visible from the water have banners but most do not—and they are still totally disorganized and pointing every which way going all the way up the hill from the beach.

Just in time I remembered what happened last time I climbed out of a dinghy over here—I stepped on a slippery rock and nearly fell on my arse. Definitely not the most dignified way to arrive. This time I was more careful when I stepped off the front of the dinghy.

******

As soon as I touched dry land I stopped and waited; and watched—and was watched. My mangled face with the marks of its crude sailor stitches certainly drew a few looks—and then somehow caused people to look away and go about their business. *Tori said I look like a ferocious wolf and had insisted I wear a new tunic and that she be allowed to wash me and trim my beard and hair.*

My arrival certainly got some initial attention both as I was rowed ashore and then when I stepped on to the beach. My face probably guaranteed that—I still look like shite and there's no half way about it.

The crusaders' camp was crowded and extensive. There were people and tents jammed together all the way up the hill from the beach. Some women too, mostly camp followers and prostitutes from the look of them.

No one in the area where I landed said a word. They just all stopped what they were doing for a few moments and looked at me as the chattering noise of their voices temporarily died away when they realised I was someone new and not one of them.

A middle aged man with streaks of white in his beard came out of a nearby banner tent tying on his codpiece followed by a slatternly woman in a peasant dress following along behind him. She looked at me with intelligent and curious eyes. I could almost hear her asking herself "who is this man?"

"Hello, I am looking for the tent of Lord Boniface," I called out to the man in Norman French as I limped a few steps towards him. "Do you know where it is?"

He just looked at me and shrugged his shoulders. He clearly did not understand a word I'd said. But then the woman behind him said something and he turned to her. Then he turned to look at me and then back to her and said something. Then he said something else and they had a brief conversation.

"He is in the building on the other side of the hill," the woman finally said in Norman French. "Sir Robert wants to know what you want with Lord Boniface."

"I have things to discuss with him," I replied with a smile. Then I added, "Do you know where his headquarters is located? I will give you a copper coin if you will lead me to it."

The slatternly woman with streaks of grey in her long hair looked at me intently for a moment and said something to the knight. He made a face and shrugged his shoulders in indifference as he adjusted his tunic to cover his codpiece—and turned around and walked back into his tent.

She had obviously asked permission and from the

gestures of the two of them back and forth it would appear he had given it.

******

"I will take you there." She said in Norman French after Sir Robert disappeared into his tent.

She led the way as we walked up the hill that ran up from the shore through closely packed tents and past smoking fires, piles of shite, and numerous cats. There were cats everywhere just as there are in the city across the way.

People looked up curiously as I limped past them and then went about their business. A few silently smiled and nodded greetings. Some of the voices in the background sounded French but many more seemed to be Italian and strange.

"You speak Norman French same as me except for the accent. Where did you learn it?" I asked my guide as I stepped over a dead cat on the ground. There were ants and bugs all over it.

"I came out with Gerard when he was one of Jermaine's men. He was from my village and I was wife to him until he and my two children died of the coughing pox last year. Since then things have not been easy. There hasn't been enough food even for the men. I'll die soon I suppose." She said it as if it didn't matter much one way of the other.

A thought crossed my mind.

"Is there any way for you to get across the water to the city?" I asked with a nod towards Constantinople's walls.

We could see them clearly from where we were walking on the side of the crowded hill.

"I went over to the city four or five times looking for food but the guards wouldn't let me in. I have nothing to give them except myself and they weren't interested—there are others younger and prettier than me."

We were in a little open space when I stopped. "Wait," I said quietly with a tone in my voice that caught her attention immediately. She stopped and looked at me.

"Do you know the gate by the quay where the English moor their galleys and cogs? Could you come to it once a week?"

"No. But I could find it I'm sure. Why do you ask?" She looked at me suspiciously, very suspiciously.

"Because I am always in need of information about the crusaders and Venetians. What the men are being told; the food situation now that the Venetians have brought more; the plans, the morale, the training, arguments between them, arrivals and departures. That sort of thing."

She looked at me with great interest so I continued.

"You could pretend to be going there to lift your skirt for an old priest or merchant in the back of his church or stall. That would explain the coins you'd receive and the food you could buy and bring back."

Her eyes lit up and her hand flew to her mouth.

"I could do that. Yes, I could." She said it with a strange determination. "I don't owe this lot a thing. Not a thing."

We stood in the little open space on the hill and talked for some time as we arranged things. *She's sharp as a*

Damascus blade, this one is.

We soon settled on a generous price for her services— she is to go to the city via the English gate at least once per week, and more often if there is important news; for that she is to receive a silver coin for each visit she makes and a free trip to Cyprus or back to England if we leave or she is discovered.

Before we started up the hill again I gave her two silver coins from the little pouch on the leather belt I tie around my Egyptian gown.

From what she told me that would be more than enough for her to feed and clothe herself and to find a tent to share without having to take a man unless she wants one.

"If you do want a man, try to find a servant of Boniface or of one of his lieutenants who is close to him."

"I was already thinking about that," she said. "By the way, my name is Jeanette. I was berthed in a village near Rennes. Who are you?"

"William is my name," I told her. "Just William; I'm from Cornwall."

Chapter Nine

Our new recruit.

Jeanette and I walked together up and over the little hill and started down the other side. It was just as crowded with tents and people and smouldering fires on this side of the hill as it was on the side nearest to the water where we met.

I stopped walking when Jeanette pointed out what she thought might be Boniface's quarters. It was a small stone hovel with a crusader flag on a pole and a guard standing at the door. A couple of hobbled horses were near it; their ribs were showing and they were scrounging the ground for blades of grass.

"I'll go on from here alone and walk back to my dinghy when I'm finished. Keep watch on the dinghy. If I don't return to the dinghy by four hours after the sun comes up tomorrow morning I want you to go as soon as possible to the English quay and ask for Lieutenant Henry. He is to be told everything you know or hear or think."

"Tell Henry that William said that in the name of Bishop Thomas and William's son George he is to immediately give you one silver coin and an additional silver coin each week for whatever information you bring about the Venetians and the crusaders—and remember that even having nothing new to report is important information for Peter to know." *I don't know why but somehow I feel I've done something good in finding Jeanette.*

"Bishop Thomas and William's son George." she repeated the names several times to fix them in her mind. "Yes I can do that."

I gave a little farewell nod to Jeanette and limped rather cheerfully down the muddy slope to the little stone building.

As I got closer I could see that it looked like a shepherd's hovel with mud daubed into the cracks between the wall stones and moss and green plants growing out of the slate stones on top of the roof. It had a low entrance without a door and one small window with a wooden shutter. A cat was sunning itself on a rock by the entrance.

"Hello," I said to the man standing by the entrance as I walked up. "I'm Captain William of the Pope's poor landless sailors and I am here to see Lord Boniface."

He looked at me with every indication he couldn't understand a word I said and then shouted something over shoulder to someone inside. A few seconds later a young man poked his head out of the door to look at me; I repeated what I'd told the guard, both in Latin and in Norman French.

"You are Captain William of the English galleys?" the young man inquired with an absolutely astonished look on his face.

"The one and only at your service." I said it with a slight bow, a friendly smile, and a nod of my head.

He started to say something and then shook his head as if to clear cobwebs from it and gave me an intense and disbelieving look before he darted back inside. There was some loud talk and an older man came to the door and then stepped outside. The young one was behind him and looking over his shoulder as he addressed me.

"You are William, the captain of the English?" He was plainly suspicious. Whilst I was answering with a smile and a nod he was looking around to see if I was alone.

My questioner was a large man with a dirty food stained beard. He was hatless and wearing the pants and embroidered shirt of a French noble. He was not wearing any armour.

"I have that honour," I replied with a nod of my head and another little bow of acknowledgement and smile. And who might you be? Are you Boniface of the crusaders? You have a very nice shirt, by the way."

"My name is Henri of Hainaut. I am one of the commanders of the Flemish crusaders."

I understood his name because he thumped his chest when he said Henri and Hainaut, but no more. It soon became clear that we need an interpreter.

 A terse order to the guard sent him scurrying off whilst Henri and I and the other young man just stood and stared at each other. A few minutes later the guard returned with an older white bearded man, obviously a hastily summoned priest. He hurried up wearing a big wooden cross around his neck and some kind of grey robe I'd never seen before.

"Who are you?" the priest demanded in some strange tongue. At least that's what I assumed he'd said.

I couldn't understand him so I replied in Latin. "I am William, captain of the English archers and Master of the Pope's Order of Poor Landless Sailors. I am here to speak with the leaders of the crusade about refugees and coins."

These men are crusaders so I decided to use the papal title Thomas bought for me. Not that I expect crusaders to be religious but one never knows. Perhaps the priest is religious. Some of them are you know.

Lord Henri and the priest chattered away to each other for quite some time; they periodically stopped talking and looked at me and then resumed. Both of them waved their hands around quite a bit as they spoke.

"Why are you here and how did you get here?" the priest finally inquired in Latin.

"I came on the English war galley anchored on the other side of the hill. I came to make the same kind of arrangement with the crusader leadership we made and honoured at Zara—to carry refugees from Constantinople in the event the crusaders resume their siege. It is best if these things are arranged in advance."

Yes, I know—I may be encouraging the crusaders to renew their attack on the city to earn coins from the refugees who will then flee. Of course I am; that's what we do to earn our coins isn't it?

I don't know what Lord Henri thought of my explanation but my announcement of a nearby English war galley seemed to shock both men. His lordship shouted something at the guard who promptly dashed up the hill, undoubtedly to look.

A few minutes later the red faced and wheezing guard returned and with much excited talking and arm waving that apparently confirmed my statement.

******

Lord Henri left almost immediately—"to talk to his friends," the priest explained. That was fine except that it left me with the priest who couldn't stop talking.

It was if the priest felt some kind of obligation to fill every moment with noise to entertain me. I've known a few such people and they don't bother me if they have something to say. Unfortunately this man didn't.

After a few minutes of listening to the priest babble on, I stopped responding and turned away to stand in the shade and piss against the wall of the hovel. When I finished I ignored the priest and looked at the camp—and he kept talking the entire time.

Finally, when I realised the priest was beginning to describe the icons in some church somewhere, I broke into his stream of words and told him "to shut the fuck up." It worked.

Lord Henri, probably Count Henri or perhaps a count's bastard or second son, returned after I'd cooled my heels for most of a blessedly silent hour. By then I had walked around a bit and looked at the crusader camp.

For some reason the densely packed crusader camp reminded me of the refugee encampment we'd found outside the caravanserai at Latika those many years ago when the eighteen of us walked in from Lord Edmund's castle—it wasn't so much the similar chaos and smell, it was the underlying sense of uncertainty and desperation of the people in it.

******

Lord Henri returned with three men as some sort of an escort. He didn't introduce them but from their dress and the fact that one was wearing chain despite the summer heat *as I am under my tunic* they are undoubtedly crusader lords or knights.

I just looked at the newcomers impassively as they walked up with Lord Henri—and stared at me intently as they did. There were no introductions.

His lordship, or whatever Henri is, motioned for me to follow. He and the men he'd brought with him turned around without saying a word and walked with me towards large tent with a strangely shaped banner attached to it. It was some distance away from the main camp, at least a thousand paces.

It was hard to tell the purpose of the men who walked with us— it was almost as if they were guarding him from me instead of guarding me to keep me from running. That's probably wishful thinking.

By now the camp knew that something was happening even though they didn't know exactly what it might be— hungry looking crusaders and their women began to gather and stand silently on both sides of the path as we walked briskly towards a smaller cluster of about a dozen tents well off to the side of the main encampment.

The tents we were walking towards almost all had banners on them and there were a number of horses attempting to graze on the ground around them. Most of the tents were made of rough linen but as we got closer I could see that a few were leather and several were quite large. This is where I should have come in the first place.

We walked along the side of the hill and the priest translated as Henri told me he was taking me to meet the hastily assembled crusader leadership, meaning Boniface himself and some of the crusade's other commanders.

"All those who could be quickly assembled," confided the priest in Latin, "even Lord Boniface, the Marquis himself."

The priest seemed strangely excited and appeared and acted as if he was greatly impressed with himself. Perhaps he is proud of the role he thinks he might soon be playing in some great event—which, of course, it is if sacking cities and separating refugees from their coins is your goal in life.

There were a number of men standing around outside one of the larger tents as we approached. They all eyed me with a great deal of curiosity as I walked up. There were several Venetians present as well. I could tell from the foppish nature of their clothes and the open expressions of hostility on their faces.

From the way three of the men were standing it was obvious that they are more important than the others. One or more of them, hopefully, can negotiate and make decisions.

I bowed and nodded in acknowledgement as each of the three men was named to me by the priest. Good, one of them is indeed the Italian, Count Boniface. He's the swarthy one with the grey tinged beard. Boniface may not know it, but he became the leader after my brother Thomas killed the original leader of the crusade, Robert Thibaut, when he tried to stop the Pope's first letter from being delivered.

A wicked thought came to mind when I nodded to Boniface as he was named to me—maybe I should ask him for a share of his takings since we are the ones who made his larger share possible by killing his predecessor.

Then I named myself to the assembled men and got straight to the point by speaking directly to Boniface in Latin.

"I am William of Cornwall, captain of the English archers and Master of the Pope's Order of Poor Landless Sailors. I'm here to negotiate for a mutually profitable release of refugees from Constantinople just as we had with your crusaders at Zara—wherein anyone could escape from your siege if they paid."

One of the Venetians impolitely hissed out an answer before Boniface even had a chance to reply.

"You are a pirate. We should kill you."

It was a challenge; a threat I couldn't ignore.

"Hopefully Lord Boniface and his fellow crusaders are not as stupid and badly informed as you are."

That was my initial reply with a touch of insult and disdain in my voice as I looked hard at the Venetian. Then I added an explanation as the Venetian's eyes widened. He hadn't expected such a response and began to sputter out a response as I continued and talked over whatever it was he was trying to say.

"Men who want to be rich do not eat the seed, they eat the harvest—and they certainly do not commit suicide before the riches are gathered as you would have the crusaders do. Your words are against the best interests of the crusaders—they're either the words of a fool or of a traitor who doesn't care about the crusaders."

"Enough of that," a red faced Boniface roared and the priest quickly translated.

"We will listen and make our own decisions." He was clearly more than a little embarrassed by the Venetian's outburst.

And with that the red faced Italian marquis scratched the lice in his crotch and turned and entered the tent after indicating with a sweep of his hand that I should follow. Two of the crusaders entered with us and so did one of the Venetians and Lord Henri or whatever might be his title.

After a moment's hesitation the priest followed us in with his eyes constantly darting about to see if anyone was angry with his entry.

There was a bit of talking outside the tent. A few seconds later a half a dozen or more men, including the two Venetians, also followed us into the tent and took up positions standing around the rough wooden table and the six crude stools placed around it. The tent flap was left open so that the light of summer day flooded in. *I'm hot in my chain and tunic and there is no two ways about it.*

As soon as I sat down on one of the stools I wiped the sweat from my brow and the priest moved to stand next to me to translate. There were several parchment rolls on the table. Maps from the look of them.

******

"Why did you come here?" demanded Boniface after he and his fellow commanders sat down and the rest of the men arranged themselves to stand around the table. "These Venetians here say it is to spy on us?" *It may have been my imagination but Boniface and the others all seemed to be staring at my recently wounded neck and face as he spoke.*

"I don't need to spy on you or the Venetians. I already know how weak the Venetians are and I know you still don't have enough food to get through the winter and I most certainly know what it is most of your crusaders want—I've been a crusader myself, haven't I?"

That was my answer as I tapped the little crusaders' cross sewed on my tunic. I leaned forward and raised my hand in a non-threatening way to make my point as I repeated what I'd already said several times today.

"My purpose in coming here, my only purpose, is to work out a mutually good contract between us wherein we all fetch as many coins as possible from the refugees if and when your crusaders resume their siege—a contract between us such as we had at Zara."

We then spent quite some time discussing Zara and the various possible details such a contract might contain for Constantinople—and ended up with everyone nodding tentative agreement to something very similar to that which we had at Zara:

At the end of each day the crusaders are to get five silver coins for each refugee our galleys have boarded that day; we are to have exclusive use of our current quay and the gate in the city wall near it. No crusader or Venetian attack is to be launched on our quay or the section of the city wall next to our concession and no effort is to be made to hinder our crews or our galleys or the departure of the refugees.

"I am surprised at your request, Master William. I would have expected you to ask that we go to the Holy Land as the Pope desires or for a share of the gold coins we are to receive from the new emperor. And what if we don't agree or the Venetians kill you?"

I leaned forward and looked directly into Boniface's eyes as I spoke with great sincerity and a twinge of sadness, but no hostility.

"My men and I have no interest in the lands of the empire. We are content with the lands we have in England. Coins and gold, of course, are another matter. We always need them to pay our men. But waiting for the coins and gold that you may or may not get from the emperor's treasury is another matter. My men are used to being paid promptly—so we would prefer the certainty of some coins now from the refugees to the uncertain chance of more coins later from the emperor." *Don't they know the treasury is empty? Or is it?*

"And as for me being killed? Well that's another matter entirely. If it happens, you and your men and all the Venetians will die here or worse, every one of you. That much I know to be an absolute certainty."

Then I leaned forward and deliver my threat with a sad and apologetic smile so he wouldn't take offense.

"If I don't return my men are under orders to immediately destroy the Venetian fleet anchored next to your camp—which means, of course, you and all your crusaders and the surviving Venetians will be trapped here until most of you die of starvation or are sold to the Moors as slaves."

Boniface sat back on his stool and looked at me intently. "That's hard to believe," he finally said.

"I most respectfully suggest it is true and that you should believe it. My galleys closed both the Dardanelles and the entrance to the Black sea at dawn this morning—and they won't open them to any Venetian ship until I return and order them opened. The city will continue to get its food from the Bosporus and the Golden Horn and overland. Where will you get yours?"

One of the Venetians was outraged. "If the Dardanelles are closed, which I sincerely doubt, my galleys will open it immediately." He glared at me as he said it.

"That's not likely, but please do try." I invited him with a sad smile. "We English can always use more prizes."

I turned to the intrigued crusaders and explained whilst the Venetians fumed.

"The Venetian rowers are mostly unarmed city peasants and starving slaves chained to the rowing benches; in contrast our rowers are all experienced English fighting men, and they are all fully trained and have much better weapons than the Venetians. The result when we meet Venetians at sea is always the same—we take another prize."

I turned back to the swarthy Venetian and poked my finger at him and spoke intensely as I added a real threat.

"Oh yes, there's something rather important that I forgot to mention, Signor whoever you might be; destroying your fleet so that *you* strand the crusaders here without food is only the *first* thing my Englishmen will do if there is no agreement or my return is delayed. When my men finish destroying your cargo tansports and galleys in these waters they'll be sailing for Venice itself—to capture or burn all the shipping in the harbour and sack Venice itself."

I leaned forward, put on my best winning smile, and opened my arms in warmth to those sitting with me around the table.

"But why should we make threats and fight among ourselves when we can make an honourable agreement that lets good Christians and Jews escape from the fighting and immediately brings additional gold and silver coins to us all—including the Venetians?"

******

Reason and the promise of immediate coins prevailed. Eventually even the Venetians reluctantly agreed to allow our galleys to carry refugees in peace. They agreed rather quickly once Boniface and the crusaders picked up on my threat regarding their galleys and transports and expanded it.

"If you fight the English and lose it will be very hard for the Venetians who survive. My men will surely be unhappy about being abandoned and hungry. It is doubtful I'd be able to save you and your men even though, of course, I would try."

I suspect it also helped when I mentioned that, even though we English were not willing to take sides and had no interest in sharing the resulting land and loot, "we are always willing to carry anyone to safety or to the Holy Land if we are at peace with them—even crusaders."

I did not, of course, mention that they would have to pay in advance and that I was aware that very few of the crusaders had any coins left.

Chapter Ten
William

My slow and limping walk back to my dinghy with Boniface and his nobles turned into quite a procession in the searing summer heat. We're partners in the picking of Byzantine purses and temporarily at peace even if we aren't friends. The camp inhabitants smiled their approval from their shelters and nodded as we passed. News travels fast in a densely packed camp.

Jeanette was nowhere in sight and neither were the Venetians even though we could see their cogs riding at anchor and their galleys pulled up on the nearby beach.

My little two man crew of dinghy sailors saw me coming and quickly pushed the dinghy out into the water for an immediate departure. I bowed and made my farewells to Boniface and his entourage and stepped very gingerly into the gently rocking little boat. We left immediately and I had my chain mail stripped off before we got ten paces from shore.

As I climbed into the dinghy I realised I have a terrible fear of being drowned—and resolved to never again climb over the railing of a cog or galley wearing chain mail. I also realised I was incredibly hot and sweating.

******

Tori and my lieutenants Harold and Peter were relieved to see me and we got underway as soon as the two sailors and I climbed aboard and the dinghy secured. Both of my lieutenants had advised against my going into the crusader camp. They feared I'd fall afoul of the Venetians who apparently share the camp. That hadn't turned out to be my big problem; it was the summer sun and heat that nearly did me in.

"For god's sake get me something to drink. The sun has made me weak."

The very first thing I did was alert Peter that an important woman would be reporting in every week or so—and that he should tell the sergeants in charge of the gate that people asking for Lieutenant Henry are to be treated with respect and their reports taken very seriously.

Peter is to pass the word to all the men stationed here that any woman asking for Lieutenant Henry and mentioning Bishop Thomas and William's son George is to be at all times protected and treated with great courtesy.

"And please make sure they understand that she is one of ours no matter how she looks or how she's dressed."

I described Jeanette but did not mention her name— and told Peter and Henry to never ask for her name or discuss her with anyone, only that they should pay her immediately and carry her to Cyprus or England if she ever asks to leave.

I also made sure they understood that the senior man present in Constantinople and both Peter and I are to be informed immediately each time she reports in—and that a message "nothing is new" is an important message and is also to be reported.

Then for some reason I was suddenly very tired.

******

The sun shining in my eyes through the doorway woke me up. I opened my eyes and struggled to sit up. At some point I realised I was on a string bed and covered with a light linen sheet. A rolled up rain skin had been stuck under my head as a pillow. *Where am I? How the hell did I get here? And why is the sheet so wet?*

Tori was asleep next to me and giving off little snores. The slight motion of the floor told me I was on a ship that wasn't moving. Of course, this is front castle on Harold's Galley where Tori and I live.

My movement woke her. All of a sudden Tori snorted loudly through her nose and sat up.

"You're awake! Oh thank God; we've been so worried that Harold sent for the Greek healers. How do you feel? Are you thirsty? Hungry? What can I get you?"

"My head hurts and I feel weak." ... "Can you get me the piss pot. I desperately need to piss. What happened? Where are we?"

"You're in Harold's galley. We carried you straight here when you fell down and went to sleep whilst you were talking to Peter. Everyone thought you'd been poisoned when you were in the crusader camp. The Greek healer came and looked at you. He said, you were probably out in the sun too long and we should pour sea water on you and let you sleep in the shade."

******

Jeanette came to the gate just after sundown with a significant report. The crusaders have finally learned that the Byzantine treasury is empty – they know there is no gold in the treasury to pay them as they had been promised by the new co-emperor. They are very angry and are arguing with each other and the Venetians about what they should do next.

******

Constantinople was on edge and there has been almost daily riots and fighting between the Greeks and Latins for more than a week and also between the supporters and opponents of the emperors. It's been that way ever since it was revealed that the crusaders had been promised a huge payment for helping the two co-emperors regain the throne and that it can't be paid because the treasury is empty.

At the moment Peter and I are standing in the moonlight and watching as one of our heavily loaded galleys pulls away from our quay with the familiar sound of its rowing drum and the swish and splash of its oars biting into the water.

With all the riots it's no surprise that there has been a significant uptick in the number of refugees seeking passage on our galleys. It explains why I'm standing on our quay watching one of our galleys leaving for a run down the Byzantine coast to deliver fleeing Orthodox merchants and priests to the port of Piraeus, the port which serves the great city of Athens.

A second rowing drum began less than a minute later and we could hear distant shouts coming from one of our galleys anchored just off our quay. It is coming in to take the recently vacated space. In a few minutes it will begin loading refugees bound for the cities surrounding the Black

Sea.

There are a lot of people lined up along the city wall waiting to board our galleys. Piraeus, the port of Athens, is the most popular single destination for those of the Orthodox faith fleeing the city. Constanta on the Black Sea, on the other hand is a popular destination for the Latin Catholics as is Rome and also Venice now that we've established a truce with the Venetians and are once again willing to sail there.

We even had to change our sailing schedule and destinations. Up until yesterday most of the refugees were Orthodox-believing merchants and priests fleeing to Piraeus and other Greek ports to get away from the crusaders. Now they are primarily the remaining Venetians and other "Latins." They are once again fleeing to get away from the unhappy followers of the Orthodox Patriarch.

Venice is where the other galley loading at the quay will be heading as soon as Martin and his men finish collecting the refugees' coins and loading them. We always charge a bit more for Venice.

******

Jeanette was here this evening just after sundown with another significant report. The crusaders and Venetians are mightily unhappy about not being paid. They are considering several courses of action and arguing about which one to pursue.

A few of them want to give up pursuing Constantinople's ever more distant gold and go on to the Holy Land even if they have to travel by land and fight

Saladin and his Kurds to get there.

Most of the crusaders, however, are arguing whether to pursue the old emperor to some city where he is thought to have taken refuge with the gold whereas others want to turn Constantinople into another Zara—they want to attack the city and sack it to get the wealth they've been promised.

The young co-emperor, whose name is also Alexios by the way, has offered to go with the crusaders to retrieve the gold from the deposed emperor and to use his navy to carry them to where the gold is believed to be if the Venetians won't. He says he now knows how much gold the old emperor took with him and it is even more than he first thought. He also promised to top that higher amount up with additional taxes collected from the city and the rest of the empire.

Jeanette thinks they will go after the missing gold because the Venetians have offered to help transport them to Thrace where the emperor and the gold are known to be hiding. *I don't blame the crusaders for using the Venetian transports; the emperor's galleys and cogs are all old and rotting worm eaten hulks. If they were loaded with crusaders they'd be more like to sink than make it out of the harbour. I wonder if the crusaders know that.*

"Harold, do you think the crusaders know about the condition of the emperor's galleys and transports and how few sailors they have?"

******

At the moment we are waiting for the last couple of men, two black robed Orthodox priests, to join us so we can begin walking to Constantinople's huge covered market. The priests live nearby and are paid to accompany us and act as translators. We use them whenever we visit the city's market to buy supplies and meet with the merchants.

The priests are working for us in exchange for the coins they'll need to evacuate their families and set themselves up somewhere where it is safer. We don't actually need the priests as translators, of course, because the merchants all speak many languages; we need them because the presence of the priests signals to the mobs of Orthodox believers that we are friendly and shouldn't be attacked.

These past few days Peter and I have only passed through the refugee gate and entered the city when we were accompanied by a dozen or more heavily armed archers and a couple of 'friendly' Orthodox priests—because the local people are unhappy with being besieged once again by the crusaders and Venetians and have once again begun killing "Latins" and rioting against the two co-emperors because of their promises to the crusaders.

The violence and rioting started last week when the crusaders resumed their siege and the people and their priests and the Varangian Guards finally found out that the treasury had been emptied by the departing king before he sailed off into exile.

It got worse a couple of days ago when it was revealed in the Orthodox churches that the crusaders were besieging the city because they had not been paid the huge payment they'd been promised for helping restore the deposed emperor and his son to the throne.

It didn't take the people and their priests long to realise that the emptied treasury meant that paying the crusaders and Venetians to end the siege would require huge new taxes to be levied on the city and the church. They are, not to put too fine a point on the quill writing the story, greatly pissed.

Worse for the two co-emperors, it also didn't take the Varangians long to figure out that the empty treasury meant that there would be no coins or gold available to pay them their wages or buy their food.

Indeed, the hostility of the people and the Varangians towards "Latins" and the co-emperors had become so serious that there was a rumour going about that the young co-emperor Alexios IV has fled to the crusader camp for safety.

******

The hostility towards anyone who does not speak Greek is now so bad that I even removed my little 'crusaders cross' from my Egyptian gown before I surrounded myself with archers and priests and went to the market with Peter to meet with some of the merchants.

It meant very little to me; I only had Tori sew it on in the first place because I thought it might help soothe Boniface and his men.

We received a few hostile looks as we walked through the lanes to the meeting but no one was foolish enough to attack us. Even so, there was enough hostility in the air that I informed the merchants and refugee brokers we were meeting that this would be our last visit into the city to meet with them and visit the market until things improve. Anyone who needs a meeting or wants to sell us something in the future will have to meet us at the gate in the city walls where the refugees assemble to board our galleys and cogs.

******

Everything just changed. A truce has been arranged between the crusaders and the city and the siege has lifted. The number of refugees is sure to decline at least temporarily. Maybe the worst has passed for them; and the best has passed for us.

There is a truce because some of the crusaders are going to Thrace with the young co-emperor to capture the emperor who escaped with the gold. Their intention is to bring the missing gold back to Constantinople and use it to pay the crusaders. The city and the church have agreed to this because it means the new taxes will stop being collected.

The only problem is a big one even though no one seems to know it—there is no gold for the emperor's son and the crusaders to find and bring back. They don't know it yet and we're not about to tell them. The Venetians obviously don't know it either—in return for a bigger share of the gold they've agreed to carry the co-emperor and six thousand crusaders to Thrace. That's where the emperor is thought to be sheltering with the missing gold.

"How long do you think it will take the crusaders and Venetians to figure out that there is no gold?" Peter asked me.

"I have no idea but I would think it likely it will take quite a while. If it looks like the truce is going to hold, it might be a good time to redeploy some of our galleys by sending them out full of refugees and then having them continue on to be used elsewhere—and for Harold and Henry and I to spend some time on Cyprus."

Then I paused and grinned and raised my chin towards Peter.

"And that means, my dear friend, that you'll have to stay in command here so we get useful reports and our post captain doesn't get us into trouble—Martin's a useful sergeant and steady as a rock but sometimes he's a bit slow on making decisions, isn't he?" *And the big problem is that neither Martin nor you can read and write.*

******

We organized our departure and two days later Peter Sergeant and Martin Archer were on the quay waving goodbye and wishing us well as we rowed out of the harbour on Harold's galley bound for Cyprus. The autumn winds were favourable and the sea storm free. We reached Cyprus in early October.

Our welcome was warm as usual and what we found was very reassuring—Yoram has continued to get excellent results as the post captain and so have the senior sergeants who stepped in for Harold and Henry whilst they were away. Everyone stared when they thought I wasn't looking but no one asked about my face and limp. They'd already heard how it happened from the men coming in on galleys from Constantinople.

Within hours we'd all settled into our regular routines. It was almost as if we'd never been away and the next few weeks were among the best of my life. Tori was particularly pleased to be back in Cyprus. She absolutely adores Yoram's wife, Lena, and their ever growing brood of children.

******

Big surprises are the order of the day today. One of the galleys based in Cornwall came in with an alarming message from Thomas. He reports both the crops and the fish have failed in Cornwall and starvation is looming in the villages. He is going to release our siege stores and food reserves but even that may not be enough. His request is simple—please send all the corn, dried fish, and olive oil you can buy as quickly as possible.

I responded with an emotional letter telling him that I remembered all too well being a hungry serf as a boy and our mother starving and that no one was ever going to starve to death in Cornwall if I had anything to say about it. I assured him we would begin shipping food immediately and it would keep coming until everyone was fed and we'd had built up much larger reserves than ever before.

We had no more than put together a plan to help Cornwall when three galleys full of refugees came in one right after another with reports from Peter in Constantinople. The truce has totally broken down and the fighting and rioting in the city is more intense than ever— between the Greeks and the Latins and between the supporters of the co-emperors and those who oppose them. Peter wants us to send all of our available galleys and cogs to evacuate refugees.

The situation in the city sounds desperate and thus full of promise. So I decided to go to Constantinople myself and take Henry with me. Harold and Yoram will stay in Cyprus to buy the food supplies and get them on their way to Cornwall even though it means sailing during the storm season and paying to charter cogs.

Getting food to our people in Cornwall, I told them, is our highest priority; much higher than getting galleys and cogs to Constantinople to transport refugees.

My initial plan was for Tori to stay here with Yoram and Lena whilst Henry and I were in Constantinople. That lasted until I told Tori my plan. Ten minutes later a new decision was reached—she's coming with me.

"Famines and fighting and archers I can handle; women are beyond me."

I said it ruefully to my smirking lieutenants as Tori triumphantly marched out of the hall to begin packing our things for an immediate departure. Then we went back to our lists of galleys and cogs and sergeants and resumed our planning.

Several things are certain—one is that in the future we're going to have to maintain much larger food reserves in Cornwall. Another is that we're going to have to recall the galleys we just took away from Constantinople and send them all back and then some. We'll need more galleys because most of our cogs, even the pirate takers, will have to carry corn and other food to Cornwall.

"And here on Cyprus, Yoram? Do you have enough food reserves for an extended siege? Do you think you can safely spare any for an immediate shipment on the cog we have in the harbour?"

******

Our return passage to Constantinople was fast and it was a dark and overcast day as we rowed past the fishermen lining the shore and moored at our quay. We were in Harold's superbly equipped and crewed galley with his senior sailing sergeant and pilot, Geoffrey, in command. Harold himself reluctantly stayed in Cyprus to reorganize our galleys and cogs and sergeants so as to get food on its way to Cornwall and more refugee carrying transports to Constantinople.

By the time we tied up at the quay things were even more desperate than Peter had initially reported. The young co-emperor has quit searching for the missing gold and returned to the city empty handed.

The co-emperor, and perhaps he alone, understands how weak the city's defenses have become and the threat posed by the crusaders. He had been there and seen them sack the cities of Thrace as they searched for the gold and, unlike most of his subjects, knew what they would do to Constantinople if they were able to breach its walls.

The younger emperor's thinking was basically sound—it is better to give up some of the city's wealth than lose it all by having the crusaders sack the city. Accordingly, he promptly ordered the destruction and melting down of valuable Byzantine and Roman icons in order to get their gold and silver and use it to pay the crusaders.

Unfortunately, not everyone in the city agreed with him or understood what would happen if the crusaders were not paid. The Patriarch of the Orthodox Church, for example, did not want the church to give up its wealth. He promptly denounced the emperor's order as "desperate sign of weak leadership that deserved to be punished by God."

The citizens and their clergy responded in force to the Patriarch's call to protect the church. They rose in full rebellion and took out their fury against the Latins and the emperors' supporters. Criminals and looters and arsonists soon joined in and no man or property was safe.

Refugees dug up their buried coins and hurried with their families to the safety of our little concession between the city wall and the water.

It was the best of times if you earn your bread carrying refugees as we do. Our turnover of refugee coins grew and grew, particularly after the Venetians began bringing the crusader army back from Thrace and the crusaders began tightening their blockade around the city.

******

Jeanette had arrived an hour or so earlier and was telling Henry, Peter, and me the latest news from the crusader camp. Her visit was a surprise because she usually arrives after dark. This time she said, she'd come earlier because she has important news—there is no question about it, the crusaders and Venetians are going to launch a surprise attack and try to take the city.

She doesn't know when or where they will attack except that they are not quite ready and it might be as much as several weeks before they are.

We were talking about the timing of the crusader attack and other things when a archer ran to us from the city gate where we had, for obvious reasons, stationed a strong force of guards. *We needed a strong force at the gate—Poor and desperate refugees had somehow gotten it into their heads that we'd carry them to safety without payment if they could get through the city gate and into our little concession between the gate and our quay.*

"A big force of Varangians are at the gate with an interpreter, dozens of them. A man who says he is their amir wants to talk to you. He says it is important."

I instinctively knew it was indeed important and immediately told Jeanette to wait and stay out of sight. I asked one of the nearby archers to take her to one of our little cooking fires next to the wall for some bread and cheese, "and some ale if she wants some." Then I motioned for some of the nearby archers to come with me and walked along the wall to the gate.

A huge and burly red faced man with grey streaked blonde hair stepped forward and gave me a hard look as I came through the gate and joined the company of archers grouped together to block the gateway. He was just inside the gate and surrounded by a dozen or more similarly big and tough looking men; obviously his personal guards. They were all wearing armour and helmets and carrying shields and hooked battle axes. Several well-dressed men who looked like important government officials were with them.

A very thin and elderly white-haired Greek stood next to the red faced man wearing a shabby robe; obviously his interpreter. He stepped forward when the big Varangian did.

"Greeting Englishman," the Varangian said. "I am Theodosius, Amir of the emperor's guards. Are you

William, Amir of the English?" He inquired quite formally.

"Greetings Amir Theodosius. Yes, I am William, the Amir of the English archers. How may my men and I be of service to you?"

And I wonder why you are being so formal, Theodosius; we've talked several times previously and even went out drinking together last week. One of the men with you or the interpreter must be a spy who will report exactly what you say and what I say. It must be important. But to whom?

"I have come to speak with you Amir William in regard to certain important matters related to the crusaders who are camped across the way."

"My men and I are honoured by your visit, Amir. We would be pleased to discuss such matters with you and would be honoured to invite you and your splendid and famous warriors to inspect the small parcel of land outside the city walls which we contracted to use to board our passengers. We would also be pleased to offer you and your food and drink in one of the tents where our men conduct their business and a few of them sleep at night. Most, of course, eat and sleep on their galleys and cogs."

We used to conduct our trade and live in one of city's wooden buildings inside the wall near the gate. We abandoned it weeks ago and turned two of our cogs into barracks when the Latins in this district started being attacked by arsonists. Theodosis already knows we once had a post inside the city walls, of course, but some of the others may not.

Theodosius and I and our men walked through the gate towards to row of tents where we sleep and eat and collect the passengers' coins. Some of the waiting refugees watched with impassive faces, others regarded the Varangians with fear and loathing. *I wondered what the hell this is all about. Oh well, I'll find out sooner or later after the formalities are completed.*

"Continue your archery practise," I ordered the archers as we walked towards the tents. They had stopped when they saw the Varangians.

Of course I told them to continue; I want Theodosius and his men to see the power of our longbows so they don't try anything stupid and find out the hard way.

******

We crowded into our largest tent and inquired about each other's health as bowls of ale and wine were brought, sipped for the sake of courtesy, and ignored. It took a while but we finally we got down to business.

"I've come to discuss several things, Amir William. First, will you tell me how you will respond to the crusaders if the Venetian transports bring them here and they try to enter the city through the harbour gate here by your camp—will you permit them to do so or join them?"

"Absolutely not, Amir Theodosius. We English are neutral have accepted a contract with the city not to do so. We are not in any way allies of the crusaders or their partners and certainly not of the Venetians."

I said it strongly whilst I looked him squarely in the eye and gestured towards my face.

"Yes, I have heard they did that to you and they paid most dearly for it. But how will you react if they come?"

"We have also made contracts with the Venetians and

crusaders. They have agreed not to attack this section of the city wall and not to in any way interfere with our transports or men. In exchange, we have agreed not to attack their transports or men to revenge ourselves for the damages they caused us. We've also agreed to share with them a small portion of the coins the refugees pay us to be taken to safety." *The same portion we give to you.*

"And if the crusaders or Venetians attack this section of the city wall or try to get in through the gate?"

"If they are foolish enough to make such an attempt, which I doubt because they know I can quickly bring in more and better war galleys and men than they have, we will fight them with all our might and throw the bodies of their dead into the sea to feed the fish—and then unleash our archers and galleys against them both here and everywhere in the world including Venice itself."

"And if they do cause us to fight we will do much more than just inflict terrible casualties on the Venetians and Crusaders who are here. It will be war everywhere and we will immediately begin taking Venetian galleys and transports both here and on every sea—and we'll keep doing it until the crusaders are stranded here and starve. We have many more war galleys and much better men than the Venetians so it won't take long. If they attack us, the Venetians will lose all their galleys and the crusaders will never leave here alive."

"The crusaders and Venetians know this, of course—that's why this gate and this section of the city wall will always be left in peace."

Theodosius nodded his acceptance of my declaration.

I hope whomever he wanted to hear me believes what I said—because it is true.

Chapter Eleven
William

Peace was certainly not on anyone's mind after my lieutenants and I met with Jeanette about a week later. She arrived with important information. As usual, she walked up to our gate in the city wall after dark and Martin Archer, the sergeant in charge of our Constantinople post, personally escorted her to us. Henry hurried up a few minutes later to listen.

Jeanette almost always arrives after dark and meets with us on Harold's galley so no one sees her face. Anyone who asks is told she is a prostitute coming to spend time with one of our sergeants she has befriended. It's believable because she looks much better than when we first met—she has cleaned herself and eaten well since she became our spy.

Jeanette gets to us very carefully so she won't be exposed as a spy. She has a boatman row her across from the crusader camp to a fisherman's wharf near a gate next to the city's great market. Then she carefully makes her way through the city's streets with twists and turns to make sure no one is following, and then approaches our gate after the sun finishes passing overhead and it gets dark. Our gate sergeant, or Martin Archer himself, escorts her to us in the dark and we meet in secret on Harold's galley.

Just before dawn she'll return to our gate and, if Martin Archer's guards report the coast is clear, slip into the city whilst it's still dark. Then in the early morning light she'll make her way back through the city street to her waiting boatman—just as she would if she had spent the night with a rich merchant or priest.

Jeanette's message this evening is important—some of the crusaders returned from Thrace rich with loot from sacking Thrace's cities. That, of course, we already knew.

What we didn't know until she arrived this evening and told us is that the returnees are encouraging the crusaders who remained behind to join them in launching a surprise raid into the city. The ostensible purpose of the raid is to "send a message" about how unhappy the crusaders are about not being paid. What the crusaders really hope, Jeanette said, is that the city will fall to their surprise attack and they can sack it.

What the returnees are telling everyone is that they learned something important in Thrace when the young co-emperor captured some of the missing emperor's servants—that the reason no one has yet found the missing gold is that it is still in Constantinople.

According to their informants, the missing gold is hidden in the one place the Greeks and crusaders would never think to look for it—in the city's one and only Moslem mosque. That's fortunate because it means the crusaders can attack the mosque and retrieve the gold without incurring the wrath of the Pope.

I was surprised to hear Jeanette say that the city has a Moslem mosque. So after she left the next morning I had inquiries made among the refugees and merchants. It's true. There is a mosque in Christian Constantinople. Apparently the Byzantine Empire includes states around the Black Sea with large Moslem populations. I hadn't known that.

******

According to Jeanette the plan is for the Venetian galleys and transports to secretly load the crusaders tomorrow night and then, when the wind is right, suddenly carry them across the water to climb the city's walls in several places using tall ladders they are making for that purpose. There is also a rumour that bribes have been paid and one of the city gates will be unguarded.

Then Jeanette told us who would be in the raiding party the Venetians will be carrying across the water— almost all the crusaders. That's when I realised that it's not a raid on a mosque that's about to occur, it's an all-out surprise attack to capture the city.

"There is something else," she said hesitantly. "I think they suspect me. One of the men I know asked me a lot of questions yesterday and I think someone tried to follow me when I left the camp this morning. That's why I was late tonight—I waited until it was dark before I left the market and then started off in a different direction. I'm sure I lost them in the dark but I'm frightened about going back."

"That's bad, Jeanette; very bad. You can't go back. The camp is too dangerous and so is the city. You'll have to stay here with us."

"Would you really let me stay here with you? Really?"

"Of course, I gave you my word didn't I?"

Then she embarrassed us and said something that had Tori smiling and Henry staring down at the rough table and looking a bit emotional.

"Oh thank you, thank you. You are truly good men. I shall pray for each of you every day for so long as I live."

After she left with Tori to get something to eat I lowered my voice and spoke to Henry who had a strange look on his face. *Jeanette had met Tori on her previous visits and was present during this one because for privacy we meet in the forward castle where Tori and I live.*

"Are you all right, Henry?"

"Yes. Of course I am. It's just that no one ever said they'd pray for me before."

******

We got to work immediately and worked all night to get the archers fed, battle ready, and in formation in front of the gate when the sun came up.

Our galleys and cogs in port were immediately ordered to send ashore whatever supplies our archers might need as well as most of their archers. When they are finished unloading, they will move to an isolated cove up the coast with a skeleton crew of rowers and guards. Peter will command our shipping anchored in the cove; Henry will stay will me as my second.

It was a busy and hectic night. Bales of arrows were laid out, pikes and shields issued, and food, water, and firewood carried ashore.

Tori wanted to stay but I put my foot down and told

her she had to be on the galley to guard our things. She started to say something, glanced at the look of determination on my face, and nodded her acceptance. Jeanette is to stay with her in the forward deck castle of Harold's galley.

After much thinking I reached a decision and sent my horn blower to fetch a parchment and quill. The unsigned message I sent to both Theodosius of the Varangians and Boniface of the crusaders was addressed to both of them by name. It was a terse message.

"This morning before dawn, and every day thereafter, the army of the English archers will be in battle formation on our concession in front of the city wall. We will destroy anyone who attacks or approaches our concession or the city wall running behind our concession."

That was the best I could do warn them both without appearing to take sides. The reality is that we do not want the crusaders to launch a successful surprise attack—the sacking of Constantinople would immediately end our highly lucrative refugee trade just as it did in Zara. It might even result in a new emperor who might end our concession.

"Martin, take a translator with you and immediately deliver this message to the Varangian guard post on the other side of the gate. Tell the Varangian sergeant that it is very important and must be immediately handed to Amir Theodosius even if he must be awakened to receive it."

"Harold, send John's galley to deliver this parchment to the crusaders across the way. Tell him to send it ashore in a dinghy and be prepared to fight and run."

******

A few hours later we stood to arms and were ready to fight when the sun came up. We soon began releasing the men to go for food and water—the wind was wrong for the Venetian transports and the sea in front of our quay was empty except for three of our galleys—two that had come in empty from Athens' port during the night to pick up more refugees and a third that had rowed in briskly with another company of archers from Cyprus. Their sergeant captains were surprised to hear that our other galley and cogs were waiting a couple of hours away because we fear an attack.

It's a good thing the three galleys arrived. We can always use additional archers in our battle formation and the galleys that brought them can help carry the growing number of refugees lining up at the city gate.

Later that very same day an elderly Orthodox bishop approached our gate as the first of our newly arrived galleys rowed away filled with refugees and the second was loading. He seemed, so the guards thought, to be repeating the word "captain" as if asking to speak to me. He arrived at the gate alone according to the sergeant who brought me the message and then brought him to me.

Bishop Apostolos and I had a strange conversation once I realised he spoke neither Latin nor French, only Greek, and asked an interpreter to join us. He seemed very nervous and unsure of himself and quite hesitant, in need of constant reassurance that I would not tell anyone about our conversation.

What the bishop revealed when we finally began talking was quite interesting. He holds some kind of position in the Orthodox Church that puts him in charge of the church's huge collection of icons and relics. According to the bishop, many of the icons are of great religious significance and value—such as pieces of the true cross and the head and right hand of Saint John the Baptist, the hand that baptized Jesus himself.

Ugh; they must surely smell most foul.

The bishop came across to me as a worried man who is greatly concerned for the safety of his priceless icons. He assured me, obviously in the belief that I would be impressed, that the Patriarch is greatly concerned as well.

He lowered his voice and leaned forward as if to whisper a great secret.

"It's the young emperor. He wants to burn them to get the gold and silver for the crusaders. In the past his father wouldn't let him but now his father is poxed with the coughing pox and getting weak."

After much dithering the bishop came to the point of his visit; he wants to secretly charter a galley to carry some religious manuscripts and icons to an undisclosed port. According to the bishop, he cannot tell me which port because they are not yet sure themselves. *Undoubtedly they are taking church treasures to safety and don't want anyone to know about it.*

He'd come to me because he'd heard the English were reliable even though we are Latins—would we, for example, carry the icons to safety in Athens?

"Of course, we will," I promptly answered. "If you

pay in advance and your icons don't smell too badly for having been dead so long—five thousand gold bezants for a galley to Athens with no more than thirty priests and their families as passengers and one hundred archers to do the rowing and keep them safe from the Moorish pirates and Venetians."

I know that's way more than the usual rate but it's for a church and they get their coins from gulling people like my mum with promises they know won't be kept. We're different; we try to keep ours.

The bishop was obviously stunned at the number of coins and my comments about the smell. He opened his mouth and leaned forward again, probably to start to bargain. But then he stopped and looked at me closely, and slowly nodded his acceptance and assured me the Church's icons didn't smell. He'll return with the coins tomorrow morning and the icons will start arriving soon thereafter.

******

We stood the archers to arms well before the first light of dawn. Everything was quiet except for the murmur of men talking in the ranks and the muffled noise coming through the gate from the long line of refugees waiting for the gate in the city wall to open. When the sun came up the gate will be opened and they will be allowed to file in to pay their coins and line up to be boarded on a galley headed for wherever it is they are trying to reach.

There seemed to be a lot more refugees than usual this morning. They'd been gathering with their possessions on the street inside the city ever since the last galley left yesterday afternoon. The Varangians in the little guard post next to the gate lined them up and kept order. *And counted them for Theodosius as they entered.* Venders circulated among them offering food and water.

Each refugee is allowed to bring on board everything he or she can carry and some of them have unbelievably huge loads. They were the usual sad and subdued group of stoic men, weepy women, and crying children. They are almost all Greeks these days. The Latins who had enough coins to leave have mostly already gone.

Some of the refugees are going to be disappointed. Only one galley had rowed in during the night. It was presently moored at our quay with a strong force of archers on its deck. It will load refugees for Athens as soon as the sun comes up and we can see for ourselves that the coast is clear. More galleys will come in from the holding area if we are not under attack. They'll also tow in the cogs we've been using as barracks for the archers if the wind is not favourable.

******

There was a shifting in our ranks and a rapidly growing sound of excited men as the first light of the day let us see across the water to the crusader camp across the way. It's little wonder the archers are excited and talking—the sea between here and the crusader camp is covered with galleys, cogs, and fishing boats, hundreds of them, and they are all headed towards Constantinople. A major crusader attack is about to fall on Constantinople.

Chapter Twelve
Lieutenant Henry

"I'm not sure they're headed this way. What do you think, Henry?" Captain William asked me as we stood on our quay with Martin and our horn blowers watched the Venetian fleet move across the water in front of us.

"My eyes aren't the best, Captain, but it doesn't look like they're coming here; it looks like they're headed around to the city walls east of us. What do you think, Martin? You've got better eyes than me."

"I think I'm happy that I'm here and we're not taking sides between the Varangians and the crusaders. A lot of people are about to die, that's what I think."

We watched carefully as the crusaders and Venetians came across the water and began moving out of sight around the end of the city wall. It was obviously a very large force but, from the looks of where they're heading, not an immediate threat to us. After about ten minutes I stood the men down and the Captain ordered Martin to let all the paying refugees come through the gate. He's to immediately board those bound for Athens and get them on their way.

******

Two hours later the Athens galley was rowing away from our quay and the city gate into our concession was being besieged by literally thousands of newly arrived refugees. That's when Martin reported the Varangians had abandoned their guard post by the gate and that things were getting out of control on the streets outside of our gate. I was sure he was right—I could clearly hear the shouting and noise coming from the other side of the wall.

I had just walked over to the cooking fire for some fresh bread when Captain William shouted at me from over by the city gate where he'd been standing.

"Lieutenant Henry, the Varangians seem to have abandoned their post. I would be obliged if you would take a company of archers and establish order on the street on the other side of the gate. Have half the company establish a line to the left for those who show enough coins to buy passage; send everyone without enough coins to the right and have the other half of the company over there to disperse them."

"Also, let anyone from Britain or Normandy enter even if they can't pay—and let me know if a group of priests shows up at the gate carrying things that don't look like what the refugees usually bring."

Sure enough, the archers were still restoring order and getting the refugees lined up for processing and loading when a procession of priests pushed its way through the crowd and approached the gate. Some of them had women and children with them and all of them were carrying boxes and paintings and crosses and such. Bishop Apostolos was with them and full of apologies.

"I'm sorry we're late. We hired some wagons but they never arrived. The stable is down there by the gate near the heathen's mosque where the fighting is occurring."

******

The Venetian transports were out of sight around the corner of the city wall when Harold's galley, with Geoffrey in command and Tori and one hundred and forty archers on board, came in to our quay just as the Athens galley was rowing out against the wind. Geoffrey comes in at about this time each day to see if it is safe for barracks cogs and any of our other transports to return for another day.

Today Geoffrey has a special task—hurry as fast as possible back to the cove where our galleys and cogs spent the night and bring back the four galleys waiting there and one of the cogs. The other cog, the big one the archers have been using as a barracks, dare not return until the wind changes—Geoffrey's galley can only tow one cog at a time against the wind and the others don't have enough rowers to pull it because they only have skeleton crews even when the passengers help with the rowing.

Bishop Apostolos sought me out whilst the priests and their families and precious icons waited along the city wall for their galley to arrive from our holding area up the coast.

"We could not bring all the icons. Some of the priests carried their small children instead. I could not blame them. And there are so many icons that even if we risk the fighting and all of us go back we cannot carry them all. Can you provide men to help us fetch them? We'll pay you, of course."

I responded quickly.

"Five thousand bezants for one hundred and sixty men and only one hundred will help carry your treasures. The others will carry only their weapons so as to be ready in case we are attacked."

He looked at me in shock when I named the price but nodded his acceptance when I added – "One hundred strong men can carry a lot of priceless icons, true?"

Chapter Thirteen
William

We formed up the men and set off into the city about thirty minutes later. I led the archers myself and walked next to the bishop with my translator. The Orthodox priests walked rather rapidly in front us behind a very young priest with a self-satisfied look on his face who was proudly carrying a large wooden cross.

It was little wonder the priests were in a hurry—their families had all wailed and crossed themselves and began praying as we set off; the priests obviously want to get to wherever it is we are going and get back to their families as soon as possible. *The priests are in front because we are friendly and I want people to see that we are.*

I decided to lead the archers myself despite Henry's strong disapproval both at me leading them and him being left behind to defend the concession and load the refugees when Geoffrey's galley returns with our refugee carriers. Strangely enough, I found myself quite enthusiastic about getting away from our little parcel of land and marching into the city with the men. My limp was almost all gone.

The priests may have been walking rapidly in a disorganized gaggle behind their cross but the two companies of archers marching behind them certainly were not disorganized. They were armed to the teeth and marching in step to a beating drum—and in a fighting column formation instantly ready to respond to an attack coming from any quarter. Marching and being ready to instantly fight is something Henry has the archers do over and over again whenever they practice fighting on land.

People and carts on the street along the wall pressed against the buildings along the way and yielded the middle of the lane running along the city wall to us. They mostly look curious and worried but not hostile as we passed. Having the priests walking up front behind the big cross seemed to be working in terms of soothing the anxious people standing along the street. *They've every right to be anxious; the city's on its way to being sacked and they have nowhere to hide.*

******

It was cold and misty as we marched rapidly along the wide cobblestone street just inside the city wall for a while. Then we turned off to the left and marched even faster along a narrow lane. That's when we began to get into clouds of drifting smoke and hear the sound of distant fighting rising and falling in the distance somewhere ahead of us.

After about a couple of miles of walking we came around a corner and marched into a cobblestoned square. It had a big stone cross in the middle of it and a horse watering trough at the far end in front of a big Orthodox church. It was quite impressive with a big onion shaped dome on its top and all kinds of shiny coloured tiles with pictures and designs on them.

A number of people and horse carts without horses were in the square when we marched into it. Most of the people were looking towards the sound of the fighting as we entered. They quickly turned and looked at us—and seemed surprised to see us. Some of them gathered up their things and quickly left; others began shouting questions and making imploring gestures at the priests.

We didn't go to the church; we followed the priests into the long stone building running along the right hand side of the square; it is, the bishop walking next to me said, the Patriarch's residence from where he and his bishops manage the affairs of the far-flung Orthodox Church and store its treasures. We didn't all go in. I left most of the men on guard outside and entered with the priests, my translator, and the small squad of archers who are my personal guards.

The priests certainly knew where they wanted to go. They didn't break stride when they turned to the right and hurried down the corridor to a large double door. It was open and we flooded into a room filled with all kinds of pictures and gold and silver crosses and jug-like things and boxes with jewels stuck in them. The priests immediately began filling their arms with all they could carry and hurrying out. Some of what they were taking are obviously quite heavy. *There's too much here; we'll never be able to carry it all.*

"Tell your priests to give what they are carrying to my men and come back for more," I ordered the bishop through my translator. He nodded and began giving loud orders in Greek. There was a note of hysteria in his voice.

In the rear of the long room there were two rows of monks and priests sitting and kneeling on the floor in front of a number of gold and silver boxes and urns of various sizes and shapes. They looked up in surprise but didn't stop their chants and prayers as the bishop and his men rushed in and began grabbing some of the boxes and carrying them out. *There really is a lot of gold and silver here; no wonder they're afraid the emperor will melt these things down.*

"What about the big gold and silver boxes, the ones you're not taking?" I asked the bishop as the last of the priests made his final trip. "Are they too heavy to move?" *Surely they are; even the small ones are heavy.*

"Oh no. We're not taking those, they're much too important to leave the city. Besides, the young emperor has said we can keep them. Since they're not in danger the Patriarch wants them to stay here to help protect the city. They contain the most important relics of all, you know—the head and hand of Saint John the Baptist, the man who baptized Jesus. It is well known that the church and the city will be protected so long as they are properly venerated. Even the young emperor knows that."

******

Almost every archer's arms were full as we began our march back to our little patch of land outside the city wall. In the end only a dozen or so archers marched at the front of the column immediately behind the priests and fully ready to fight. I unsheathed my sword and marched with the priests with the bishop and my translator and horn blower by my side. Another half dozen archers brought up the rear although they too were soon carrying icons that overly burdened priests had been forced to put down when they became too exhausted to continue.

We only had one spot of trouble on our march back towards our gate. Just before we reached the cobblestone street running along the city wall we passed through an open area with a lot of rough and hungry looking men and women standing idly in their rags among piles household goods. Most of them were very young. Looters and arsonists from the look of them, trouble makers for sure.

They watched us cautiously as the priests at the head of our column approached. Before we reached them some of them quickly gathered up their things and ran down a narrow side alley. Those who remained eyed us warily— and began talking among themselves and pointing when they saw the gold and silver on some of the icons we were carrying.

Suddenly all hell broke loose. It wasn't that any signal or command was given, to the contrary. A young man standing against the wall in the narrow lane suddenly ran into the gaggle of the priests walking immediately behind me and tried to grab a silver urn out of his arms. That unloosed a flood. Suddenly a dozen or more of the young men were among the priests and attempting to relieve them of the icons they were carrying.

I saw it all. In the blink of an eye the urn grabbed by

the young man came loose despite the priest's desperate efforts to hold on to it. The thief picked it up and started to run back down the narrow lane towards the rear of the column. He must have seen the archers marching behind the priests readying their weapons for he whirled around and ran back past the priest's grasping hands—and right into a hard slash from my sword.

I used both hands and really put my back into it. My strike hit home with such force that for a second it numbed my arm all the way up to my shoulder. I think I even heard the crunch when the sharp edge of my sword smashed into his teeth. The silver urn bounced on the cobblestones and went rolling.

For some reason I saw him very clearly as I killed him—he was a young boy, very young and very hungry and very desperate.

Behind me the priests were struggling to hold on to their icons and mostly losing them. I didn't turn back to help the priests. Instead I left the bishop's side and pushed my way through the three or four dumbfounded priests who had been walking in front of me and had to stopped to stare in horror at the melee going on behind them.

I moved ahead in the narrow lane until I got clear of the priests. Then I turned around and waited with my sword ready to take anyone who rushed at me. My horn blower, a young one striper, followed me as he should have done. He had drawn his short stabbing sword with its double edged blade when I drew mine.

"We'll hold them here." I shouted at my horn blower even though he was only a few feet away. I could see the men of my guard struggling to get through the melee to reach us.

"Don't let them get past if they are carrying anything; let them pass if they aren't."

It was over as fast as it started. A few of the robbers ran from where they were struggling with the priests to their deaths at the hands of the archers walking in the column behind the priests. Most of them, however, were among the priests and, thus, quite close to me and the front of the column.

They saw me motion a young unarmed man carrying nothing to come past me and run safely on down the narrow lane—and then one after another they began following him by putting down their swag and running past me. In the end only one tried to come past carrying something. I took his head all the way off with a heavy two handed swing.

******

"That was exciting," said the bishop as we watched the priests begin picking up the icons they and the would-be robbers had dropped. "But why did you let them get away? You should have killed them all."

I was furious and upset and I wasn't sure why.

"And you and your goddamn church should have done more to prevent them from becoming so desperate that they became robbers. Would they have been so hungry and poor and desperate if you'd taught them how to read and sum or other useful things instead of spending your time chanting prayers and accumulating coins and icons—I doubt it?"

"There will always be the poor; all we can do is pray for them."

I don't know why but the bishop's answer infuriated me. I was so upset I was beside myself with rage.

"Collecting coins from poor people and spending them on gold and silver boxes and urns doesn't sound like praying for them to me. Does it to you?" I replied sarcastically.

"It's for the glory of God," was the bishop's indignant reply. He said it with a self-righteous and rather pompous smirk.

"Glory of God, my arse. Those boys were poor and desperate; and your lot are disgraceful for keeping them that way by pissing away your time and your coins."

For some reason I thought of me mum as I said it and the look in the first boy's eyes as my sword hit him.

The bishop and I walked the rest of the way back to the English concession without saying another word to each other. All the while the priests walking behind us chattered away about the attack and what had happened to them and how they'd responded. After a while the bishop fell back and joined them.

Chapter Fourteen
William

After two days of intense fighting the exhausted and increasingly hard pressed crusaders and Venetians finally gave up on their effort to take the mosque. The crusaders had been defeated in their efforts to storm the walls but had succeeded in getting into the city by bribing the guards at a more distant gate—and then had tried and failed to fight their way through the Varangians and a host of armed and veer irate Moslem volunteers to reach the mosque. There had been many casualties on both sides.

I learned all that from Theodosius a week later when he showed up to claim his share of the coins the refugees pay us to carry them away to safety. He had been too busy to come and claim them earlier—first fighting off the crusaders who were trying to reach the mosque and then fighting the huge fire the heavily besieged and outnumbered crusaders set to cover their withdrawal.

Overall it had been a fine week of carrying refugees for us. Indeed, it was our best coin week ever because the fire burned down a full quarter of the city and many of the city's well-to-do residents finally gave up on trying to live in the city. They came to us with their families either because they had nowhere in the city to go or because they saw the sack of the city becoming inevitable. Many of the coins that went into our chests still had dirt on them from where they been dug up or pried out of hiding places.

Theodosius's share of the great flood of refugee coins was enough to fill almost an entire chest and so was the crusaders' share; ours filled more than five. But then, of course, we did all the work, provided all the cogs and galleys, and took all the risks.

The Amir of the Varangians also reported something alarming although we didn't fully realise its significance at the time—the co-emperors and their courtiers are holding on to the tax revenues that come in from the provinces. According to Theodosius, the Varangians have not been paid for two months and they are starting to get upset about it. It was, he said, the first time in living memory the Varangians had not been paid.

******

To everyone's great surprise, the city settled down considerably after the great fire and the defeat of the crusader attack. The number of refugees slacked off considerably and the Varangians were paid some or all of their arrears. The crusaders and Venetians helped matters by giving the co-emperors an additional six months to come up with the gold they were owed.

The end of the sweltering heat and the coming of cooler weather probably also helped calm things down even though it caused considerable hardship for those whose homes had burned. The combination of the increasingly cold weather and the shortage of housing was good for our refugee trade—we carried a number of refugees south to warmer ports.

It probably also helped reduce the fears of the city's residents when some of the crusaders, mostly the German knights and their men, finally gave up on ever being paid what they felt the Greeks owe them. They chartered one of our galleys and sailed for Acre to begin their crusade. Only God knows where the Germans found the coins to pay us, probably loot from the failed attack.

Somewhat similarly, a few of the merchants and wealthy families who had deposited coins with us in exchange for parchments promising they could collect a similar amount of coins at any of our trading stations, less our fee, presented their parchments and were paid.

Even the young co-emperor himself believed that some kind of corner had been turned. He left his blind and sick father and the still smouldering city to lead a large force of ever hopeful crusaders to Adrianople, one of the cities in Thrace that the crusaders had not yet sacked. Adrianople is where the gold and jewels and the missing emperor are now rumoured to be hidden.

We responded to the resulting drop in refugees and coin deposits by reducing the number of galleys and cogs and archers assigned to our Constantinople station. But we kept three companies of veteran archers there and they remained barracked on the two cogs moored to our quay instead of moving back into the tents erected on the land of our concession. We even began allowing the archers to visit the nearby taverns and whorehouses when they were off duty.

******

Henry and Tori and I left Constantinople for Cyprus on Harold's galley when the weather started to get cold and things in the city started to return to normal.

Tori and I were both looking forward to the relative warmth and comfort of Cyprus and spending Christmas in Cyprus with Yoram and Lena—both the Roman Christmas in late December and the Orthodox Christmas in early January; Henry, so he said, was looking forward to "seeing how your spy, I think her name is Jeanette," is doing in Cyprus.

"You *think* her name is Jeanette. Why you sly old dog." I teased him good.

For some strange reason I keep thinking about the boy I killed in the lane when he tried to steal and icon. It happened again as we were boarding the galley to leave for Cyprus. I was going, you see, and he was staying.

Tori asked me if having two Christmas days, one for the Roman Catholics and one for the Orthodox Catholics, is what the priests meant when they say Christ arose and was reborn. I told her I didn't know what it meant because I never understood anything when I attended church with me mum because the priest spoke only Latin—except, of course, when he was demanding coins to save her and me from one thing or another—and I thought of the boy whilst I was telling her. *Now why did I think of him again?*

I must have been in a bad mood because then Tori vexed me by asking why the priests spoke Latin in church if they knew no one could understand it. I didn't know the answer to that either.

"Ask Thomas when we get back to Cornwall. He knows about such things." I said it so curtly that she just stood there and looked at me in surprise as I walked away.

******

Cyprus is Cyprus and the people always warm and friendly. Everyone came to greet us as we rowed in and tied up at the Limassol quay. Coming down to the quay to greet arriving galleys has become a tradition. Even Jeanette was waiting on the quay as we tied up—to Henry's great and obvious pleasure although he did his best to hide it.

Henry was startled but then we grinned at each other when I winked at him and gestured with my chin towards the part of the crowd where she was standing. Ever since she arrived she has been helping Lena's with her children and living in our depot's citadel with Lena and Yoram. Lena says she thinks Jeanette wants to return to France.

******

Whilst I'd been in Constantinople a number of messages had come in for me from Thomas. The cogs returning from carrying famine food to Cornwall brought them. Things may be good for us out here but Thomas reports they are bad and getting worse in Cornwall and all across southern England. There is no doubt about it, this year's crops have totally failed and the fish catches are the smallest in living memory, not one fish in ten compared to past years.

Thomas reports that he is sending food and men to pass it out to the parishes as fast as it arrives. His students are helping because they know how to scribe and sum. George and three of the older boys, it seems, have been made up to sergeants with three stripes and sent out to distribute the emergency supplies with our older and steadiest archers as their two stripe chosen men.

Mostly the food distribution has gone well, Thomas reported, although a Bodmin monk passing out famine food at one parish and one of the archers at another had tried to sell it instead. He had their heads cut off and hung on poles so the people they tried to cheat could see justice had been done.

There was also an attack by a band of robbers on one of the food parties that was easily beaten off. Raymond's Horse Archers are patrolling the roads and hunting for those who did it.

A particularly alarming note was in Thomas's very last parchment. He reported a rider had just come in from Raymond who is at Okehampton with his Horse Archers. Raymond reported that the Earl of Devon's men have been trying to collect corn and livestock rents from the tenants and franklins on our Okehampton lands.

He also reported that two wains of food he'd sent to Okehampton for Raymond's men and the castle's parish have disappeared along with their four guards. Devon's men are suspected of being responsible but he is not sure—it could have been a band of starving men from Devon's lands or elsewhere.

"I had the messenger immediately ride straight back and tell Raymond to use whatever force was necessary to see off Devon's men. He's to catch some for questioning if he can; kill them if he can't. I'll be taking two wains of food and an entire company of archers to Okehampton in the morning. I'll write and let you know more after I arrive."

Things must be truly difficult in Cornwall—Thomas closed every parchment by asking that we send more food as fast as possible. And we damn well will.

"Peter, please ask all the available lieutenants and senior sergeants to assemble in the inner bailey as soon as possible. I have some parchments I want to read to them and orders to give."

Chapter Fifteen
William

The relative calm in Constantinople lasted through the Christmas season and into early in the next year. Then once again all hell broke loose. It started when the elderly and blind and surprisingly once again popular co-emperor unexpectedly died whilst his son was away with a force of crusaders attempting to collect taxes in the empire's distant provinces.

Rumours swept the city that the old man had been poisoned. Serious riots and fires broke out immediately and refugees rushed to board our galleys as first one usurper and then another claimed the throne.

The young co-emperor himself rushed back to the city as soon as word reached him of his father's death—and promptly got himself strangled and unceremoniously buried by the Imperial Chamberlain soon after he arrived. The chamberlain, with the help of Theodosius and his

Varangians, simultaneously disposed of several rival claimants and promptly proclaimed himself to be the new emperor. He sent word to the crusaders and Venetians that he would pay them 'soon' and asked for more time.

******

The deaths of the two co-emperors and their replacement by first one claimant and then another and finally the chamberlain, was the last straw so far as the crusaders and Venetians were concerned. They immediately once again began blockading the city and once again set in motion their long delayed plan to attack it and sack it—they were done with waiting "just a little bit longer" in response to Greek promises to pay them at some unknown date in the future.

This time it will finally be different and everyone in the city knows it. The crusaders and Venetians had been put off over and over again with promises that they would be paid if they'd just wait a little longer for the coins and gold they think they are owed. Now the day of reckoning has finally come—the crusaders and Venetians have decided to wait no longer and the Greeks don't have enough coins and gold to make even a partial payment to keep them sweet.

******

Word of the co-emperors' deaths and the renewal of the crusaders' and Venetians' blockade and their intention to take the city and sack it reached Cyprus on a galley packed with seasick refugees desperate to get away from the renewed fighting. Most of the refugees didn't want to come to Cyprus but paid to do so because it was the first outbound galley available—and then almost didn't make it when their galley got caught in a great storm that almost put it under and resulted in three passengers being swept overboard and several others dying of exposure.

The situation in Constantinople sounded so dire, and thus the potential for refugee coins sounded so great, that I immediately sent out orders ordering all of our galleys to sail for Constantinople as soon as they became available – but only our galleys.

None of our cogs were sent to fetch refugees and deposits despite the great opportunities; they have all been assigned to carry food to Cornwall, every one of them except the two being used as barracks for the archers at Constantinople. We have additionally chartered seven more cogs and sent them off filled with sacks, barrels, and amphorae filled with dried fish, grindable corn, and olive oil. More food supplies and more cogs and other transports are being sought by Yoram and every port captain.

After a bit of discussion, Henry, Peter and I sailed for Constantinople on separate galleys. Tori and I sailed with Harold on his galley. *Yoram and the senior sergeants who are Harold's and Henry's seconds stayed in Cyprus to help Yoram ship food to Cornwall and handle the reassignment of our men and galleys to Constantinople. To everyone's surprise except mine, Jeanette sailed back to Constantinople with Henry.*

******

We did not have a pleasant passage. The seas were

rough and the winds unfavourable almost as soon as we left Limassol's harbour. The heavy weather lasted until we passed through the Dardanelles. It was so bad that Tori was seasick for several days, the rowing benches were foul, and even Harold looked a little peaked. I was miserable despite Tori's best efforts to make me feel better—which were considerable and greatly appreciated.

******

Both Henry and Peter were waiting on our concession's quay when we arrived in Constantinople on a cold and rainy day late in January. How they got here before we did I'll never know, but they did. In any event, they immediately came aboard with Martin to bring me up to date about the local situation. The news is good, at least for us—conditions are very bad in the city as a result of the renewed rioting and they look to be getting even worse when the crusaders and Venetians attack. We should be able to earn many refugee coins by carrying refugees to safety and accepting deposits of coins that can be collected, less our fee, in Cyprus and elsewhere wherever we have a post.

Henry and Peter had acted on the opportunities as soon as they arrived—by the time we moored both of the galleys on which they'd arrived had already loaded refugees and sailed with skeleton crews to Piraeus.

As a result of what I heard about the situation, we immediately began unloading all of the storm-tossed and exhausted archers and sailors from Harold's galley so it could be used to carry refugees. Tori's bedding and string bed and our clothes in the forward castle and the personal items and weapons and clothes of the sailors and archers came off as well.

A skeleton crew of new sailors and archers was quickly assembled and put aboard Harold's galley under a new sergeant captain. Martin and his men immediately began loading the galley with some of the cold and bedraggled refugees huddled up against the city wall and in the tents that had sprung up all over our little concession. They can help row. Unfortunately there is no food to send with them although there is some already on board—their galley as well as Henry's and Peter's will have to stop somewhere for supplies after it clears the Dardanelles, probably Smyrna.

Harold's men and Tori and I moved into the tents that the departing refugees and crewmen vacated. Our tent, thank the good Lord, has a crude little stone bread oven in it to keep it warm. Within minutes Tori had shaken the water out of her hair, started a fire in the oven, and gotten both of us into dry gowns from one of the chests the sailors carried in—after tickling my tummy and giggling when I took off my wet archer's tunic.

I rolled my eyes, put the hood up on my leather robe, and went off in the rain to meet with my lieutenants in the forward castle of one of the cogs we are using as a barracks for some of the archers. Traveling with Tori is always more enjoyable than traveling alone.

******

Weeks passed and we continued to prosper as the war

continued without a conclusion in sight. Passengers and deposits poured into our coin chests. Moreover, and to the great pleasure of us all, our continuing efforts to carry away refugees and their coins to safety seems to have somewhat changed how our archers and sailors are seen by the local people.

We are not seen as friends by the local people, mind you, but neither are we seen as enemies. As a result, we now allow our men to go into the nearby streets and lanes during daylight hours in groups of four to visit the local taverns and prostitutes. We also allow merchants and women to visit our camp during the day. So far only two of our archers have deserted.

The continuation of a war and blockade without an apparent end in sight was good for us—our coin chests continued to be filled as our galleys came in empty and went out loaded with refugees who paid with coins dug up from under their floors or stolen or borrowed from someone else.

One reason the war dragged on to our benefit was that imperial chamberlain who became the new emperor was not a coward and neither was Theodosius who commands his army. They constantly threw the crusaders and Venetians off balance by leading the Varangians and their other forces out from behind the city walls to fight—and they were often successful because the crusaders inevitably tried to fight man to man as if they were in a tournament instead of fighting together in support of one another as the Varangians never practiced and sometimes fought and our archers always practiced and always fought.

There is a world of difference between the two approaches—the crusaders typically treat war as if it is some kind of tournament with rules—and inevitably fought individually to impress each other and their leaders with their skills and bravery; we fought as a team to kill the bastards whilst suffering as few casualties as possible.

Initially the outnumbered army of the new emperor held its own as the Varangians were joined by some of the local citizens, particularly the gentry, who took up arms for one reason or another. There was also a trickle of troops who came in from the distant cities and lords of the empire until the crusaders closed the overland and river routes. And, of course, the city was far from starving as a result of the food that was still being smuggled in overland by the city's merchants and the fish that could be caught in the very shadow of the city walls.

Everything changed near the end of March when the new emperor's forces were worn down and finally pushed permanently back inside the city walls by the crusaders.

Once again refugees began streaming out of the city desperate to pay us to carry them or their savings to safety. Where are they getting the coins to pay us and deposit with us? It seems people are everywhere digging into their floors and gardens to retrieve their buried "emergency" coins and savings or those of their neighbours.

Others who plan to stay in the city a while longer and leave later bring us substantial amounts of coins and exchange them for parchments allowing them to get a similar amount of coins at one of our distant posts less, of course, a ten percent discount for our risk and troubles.

******

The end is finally in sight. Yesterday the crusaders somehow broke through a section of the city wall and got a firm hold in one of the city's more distant quarters, the one once inhabited by the Latins. That's when Theodosius came to claim his share of the refugee fees and confirmed it.

"It's almost over, my friend. Will you keep the coins you owe me and carry those of my men who wish to leave and travel to Athens when it's time for them to go? There aren't that many left who want to go and there will soon be even fewer."

"How many men do you think it will be?"

"Only about four hundred. Some of the rest are fools who will stay and fight; others including me will open a temporary path through the crusader lines and go to the Silivri fortress inland with what's left of the gentry who don't want to become refugees or killed. Most of the others will stay in their barracks whilst the city is sacked. They'll be safe there just as we will be in Silivri because the crusaders will find more to loot elsewhere when they sack the city."

******

Theodosius's visit set me once again to thinking about the boy I killed and the icons we left behind. The icons are apparently still there at the Patriarch's residence and the priests and monks are apparently still chanting and praying around them in the belief that their efforts will somehow insure the city's deliverance from its besiegers.

For the past several weeks I've been wondering how we could fetch the icons from the Patriarch's residence before the crusaders find them and melt them down. I'd been toying with an idea and after Theodosius's visit I ran it by my lieutenants to see what they thought of it. They liked it.

It will certainly require delicate timing. We can't go after the icons too soon or the Varangians and city's religiously oriented fighters will oppose us as they did the crusaders and Venetians when they attacked the mosque. On the other hand, if we wait too long the crusaders and Venetians will get to the icons before we do and carry them off to melt them down. And should we take the priests to safety or leave them or kill them?

"Henry, please have one of our translators ask that priest who showed up yesterday at the gate if he'd like to run a few risks to earn enough coins to buy his passage when we leave, his family's passage too if he has one."

A few minutes later I called my lieutenants and senior sergeants together in one of our tents, the leather one over near the wall, and told them what we are going to do. The sergeants like it; they should because of the prize money on offer, and so will their men when they find out about it at the very last minute. They also had several good suggestions that I immediately added to my plan.

Chapter Sixteen
William

Our first order of business is to find out where the battle lines are and if the streets and lanes are open between here and the Patriarch's residence. If the battle lines have not yet reached the Patriarch's residence the icons may still be there. We also need to know whether there are any Varangian troops or gangs in the area between here and the Patriarch's residence who might fight us.

Most of all, of course, we need to know if the icons are still there—and we can't ask anyone for fear our intentions will become known. Even our archers haven't been told about the icons, only that we will be trying to rescue some merchants—and that there will be prize money equivalent to the taking of a galley if we pull it off. *All they'll ever be told even after we enter the city is that we have been hired to rescue a monastery full of priests and get them and their worldly possessions on to one of our galleys. Both are lies, of course. Loose lips sink galleys and get archers killed.*

We allow pedlars and prostitutes to enter our camp but only long after the sun comes up and they inevitably leave before it goes down in order to get safely back to their homes and protectors before the streets become dark and dangerous. Recently, unfortunately for our need for information about the fighting, there have been very few of them—they earned enough coins to purchase passages for their families and protectors and departed.

Those few who came in today told us the lanes and city squares are dangerous everywhere at night and rapidly getting worse with large gangs of armed looters increasingly assaulting people on the streets and breaking into homes and shops. Today's refugees and coin depositors told us the same thing. The great market is closed for the first time in centuries. The city is breaking down.

Finding out about the lanes and gangs and the battle lines as of last night was relatively easy. Unfortunately we need to know about tonight and tomorrow, not yesterday and last night. In the end we talked to a lot of people and learned very little except that the fighting had not reached the Patriarch's part of the city as of last night.

So was it time to make our sortie to get the icons or not? We had not a clue.

******

The question of when we should try for the icons is just now being answered after two days of anxious waiting and asking useless questions. The Varangians we agreed to carry to Athens are coming through the gate, laying down their arms as was agreed, and marching straight on to the three galleys we have waiting to carry them to Athens.

It's a good thing we have three galleys for them because many of the Varangians have their families with them and are carrying possessions. They look exhausted and many of them are wounded, some quite seriously.

Hopefully they will be too tired from rowing and too seasick to change their minds and try to take over the galleys and go elsewhere. *I'm not taking any chances. I had Harold quietly tell the galley's sergeant captains to keep them rowing to exhaustion and to at all times keep several dozen heavily armed archers guarding the forward castle where their weapons are being stored.*

The arrival of the Varangians settled the question of when we should go for the icons. It's tonight or never and even tonight may be too late if the crusaders realise the Varangians have begun pulling back and move into the sections of the city the Varangians have vacated.

******

Lieutenant Peter paraded our galley's archers when the rain stopped and asked for six volunteers for a dangerous assignment involving going into the city in the dark tonight. It will almost certainly involve fighting.

I've been Albert's chosen man for more than three years and three years is more than enough. I want to be a sergeant myself. Perhaps this will be my chance to get ahead in the company after all these years. I didn't hesitate. I volunteered immediately. So did almost everyone else. To my surprise I was selected.

Later that night I realised why I'd been chosen when the six of us assembled in front of Lieutenant Peter's tent—all six of us had been with Captain William at the front of the column when we accompanied the priests to rescue the icons.

Candles were flickering when we entered. Both Lieutenant Peter and Captain William were present along with two Orthodox priests. I recognized them both—they'd been hanging around the camp all week and acting as William's and Peter's interpreters.

"Do you know why you were selected?" Captain

William asked.

He was surprised and seemed pleased when I spoke up.

"I believe I do, Captain—we all walked with you at the front of the column that went with the priests to get their baubles last week."

"Exactly so. Very good. What's your name corporal?"

"Roger, Captain; son of Richard the miller's helper from Crawley. Six years service, Captain."

"Well Roger Richard's son, do you think you can remember enough of how we got there and back to do it again?"

"Yes, Captain I believe I could." *Not really; all I remember is walking along the wall.*

"How about the rest of you? Do you remember too?"

Ten minutes later and we understood what we are to do and were ready to go. We're going to be in the advance party with Lieutenant Peter and one of the priests as an interpreter. The rest of the archers under Captain William will follow some distance behind us. Tom from number seven company who was a fisher from some fishing village on the York coast and I will be the runners if any messages have to be sent back to Captain William.

We're going to be out front and lead the way to the big building where we found all the priests praying and carried away some of their baubles. When we get there we're going to carry away more of their pots and boxes and such. This could be dangerous; we're the ones who'll make contact with the enemy if contact is made. I hope someone remembers how to get there and back—I sure as hell don't.

******

Martin closed the city gate and Henry inspected the men who will be going after the icons with us soon after the last galley full of Varangians pushed off from our quay. Every man is fully armed—longbow and twenty arrows, a galley shield, and either a sword or a bladed pike.

It's cold and getting colder so before he sent them back to the tents Henry also made sure that every man's long leather galley robe and its hood was dry and that every man had good sandals and a scabbard for his sword so he could keep his hands warm under his robe. Several men were shouted at by the sergeants and replaced for one reason or another.

To my great surprise and pleasure, we will be adding three Varangians to the main column. Henry asked the Varangians as they were boarding to go into exile if any of them would like to make their marks on our contract and join our company. Three of them agreed. One of them will go with Peter in the advance party; the other two with me in the main column.

I suspect they are troublemakers and the Varangians will be pleased to see the back of them. But they could be useful if we run into any Varangians or city forces tonight or in the morning.

We are taking all four of the wagons we quietly accumulated over the past few days in preparation for tonight. They'll be pulled by our pike men and be used to carry the icons we retrieve and any casualties we might suffer.

****** *Roger from Crawley*

Lieutenant Peter led the six of us and our interpreter priest out the gate in the middle of night. It's a bitter cold night and we're all bundled up with our hands inside our robes to keep them warm. What's really cold are my damn ears. That's because we're all of us wearing those funny Varangian pointed hats instead of using the hoods on our robes. The sergeant says it's supposed to make people who see us think we're a file of Varangians when we walk past them in the dark.

And of all things a Varangian with a shield and an axe came with us to make it nine of us. The poor sod can't speak a word of English but the lieutenant said he's made his mark on the company list and would be useful. So that's that; he's one of us even if he doesn't know how to use a bow and talk proper. I nodded at him and so did my mate Jem.

There were a number shivering refugees waiting at the gate when we opened it and slipped quietly out into the cobblestoned lane that runs all along the city wall. The lieutenant put his finger to his lips and motioned the refugees to enter our compound as he'd told us he would. One of Sergeant Martin's men, led them in. *We weren't going to leave them outside to spread the word; Lieutenant Peter told us that as we huddled around the little oven to eat and get warm whilst we waited nervously for the order to go through the gate and enter the city.*

The refugees were quite happy about the gate opening and being allowed to enter with their bundles even though it was still dark. Several of them started to say something and then stopped in mid-sentence as they somehow caught the tension that lay heavily in the air. As we slipped through the gate they hurriedly and silently followed their beckoning guide in past Captain William and the silently waiting three abreast column of archers behind him.

It was very dark as we turned right and walked on the cobblestone street running along the city wall. We've got a candle lantern but we didn't light it as we walked slowly and in a single file one behind the next. The priest came first, then the Varangian, and then the Lieutenant. The first two are in front to respond to inquiries and challenges; the lieutenant is the third man in our line so he can tell them what to say. I was assigned to come last and guard the rear. It's an important position and I'm determined to do it well.

We could barely make out the outline of the high city wall on our right and the buildings on the left side of the lane. As we walked I could sometimes hear the murmur of people talking and every so often catch a vague outline of someone standing or sitting along the street or walking towards us.

I don't know about the rest of the men following Lieutenant Peter, but I drew my sword and got a good grip on my shield as soon as I walked through the gate. My Varangian cap feels funny to wear but if I must wear it, I must. If only my mother and father could see me now.

******

We were trying to walk quietly and I'm always either walking backwards or with my head turned so I can see if anyone is coming up behind us. Despite our best efforts to be quiet it seemed to me as though we were making a lot of noise as we moved over the cobblestones with the high city wall looming over us on our immediate right.

Everything went as smooth as new butter until we stopped and a low whisper from the man in front of me said we may have reached the lane where we would turn to our left and move away from the wall. *May have reached? May have reached? Are we lost?*

Loud voices and arguing suddenly came out of the night from the front of our little patrol. I think I recognize it as Greek but I can't understand a word of it. Trouble for sure. I instinctively raised my shield, tightened my grip on my sword, and began backing slowly and quietly towards the voices at the front of our little column. It's my job to guard our rear.

The hair on my neck and arms rose when I heard footsteps, many footsteps, pounding towards us on the cobblestones we'd just travelled—and coming right at me Someone's been attracted by the shouting. Many a lot of people it sounds like from all the talking and shouting. *Damn I wish I could see what is happening and I wish I had a pike I could hold out in front of me and I wish I hadn't volunteered.*

Suddenly I heard a sound; a large cracking thud up to the front where the priest was walking and there had been voices. Then more thuds. Stones. They're throwing stones. That's what it is. Someone's throwing stones.

There was loud calling out in what must have been Greek from someone in our party. *Probably the priest or Varangian.* Then a lot of shouting back and forth.

"Keep moving. It was a misunderstanding. Some of the boys in this district thought we were a gang of robbers." Said Lieutenant Peter loud enough for me to hear.

Everything was alright until we moved off the cobblestone street and turned into a narrow lane. *I hope it's the right one.* It was even darker and I had to walk slower because the lane was so narrow. I'd slung my shield long ago and was walking very slowly with my hand out in front of me. I could barely see and I didn't have any idea where we are. Then it happened. I suddenly realised I was alone. I couldn't hear or see anyone.

"Hello. Lieutenant. Where are you?"

There was no answer.

****** *William*

I slowly counted to one thousand times to give Peter and his men a fifteen minute head start and then began moving through the gate and on to the street that runs along the city wall. I walked at the front of the column with the priest and the two Varangians who have joined us. Henry marched at the very rear and is in command of the second company; I'm at the very front in command of the first company.

Yes, Henry came with us; he insisted it was his place to be with the men if there might be fighting on land, particularly since we had no idea of the direction from which an attack might come.

It was slow going in the darkness and the sound of the feet of the walking men and the cart wheels on the cobblestones behind me seemed to echo off the tall city wall whose outline I could barely make out on my right side. It quickly became apparent that we should have brought at least one candle lantern for the head of the column; we're moving much too slowly in the dark.

We walked and walked and walked and the going got even slower as a cloud blotted out the faint light coming over the wall from the moon. Suddenly one of the priests gasped and whispered excitedly to our interpreter.

We've gone too far; we missed the turn.

****** *Lieutenant Peter*

There are lights up ahead and a dull flickering red glow of a fire in the sky behind them. Someone is walking with a candle lamp. I stopped instinctively to look and could hear a brief rustle in the darkness behind me as one of my men bumped into another.

"We made it," whispered the priest. "That is the Patriarch's residence. Someone is going in," he added unnecessarily.

As we watched the light suddenly blinked out as it was carried into the building whose dim outline I could see in the moonlight.

"Forward," I whispered. "and no talking."

A few minutes later we approached the building. There was a faint smell of smoke in the air even though the wind was blowing in the wrong direction to bring the fire's smoke to us. As we came into the square it was obvious that there are people in it. Now we can see them more clearly. Refugees, perhaps from the nearby fire whose glow is helping us see. So far no one has paid any attention to us except for the rock throwing incident. *Thank God they aren't someone's soldiers.*

I headed straight for the building outlined against the

glow in the sky. I remembered that the entrance is right in the middle of the building so that's where I led my little band. And miracles of miracles, there is no sign of crusaders or anyone else.

We walked up the five stone steps to the door into the Patriarch's residence and gathered around it. I quickly counted my men—one is missing. No time to worry about that now. I tried the door. It was locked. *Damn; now what?*

"Get ready," I whispered to my little band gathered in front of the door. "We're not going to wait for our main force. I'm going to knock. We're going to try to get in. Don't hurt anyone if you can avoid it."

I used the handle of my sword and gave half a dozen insistent hard raps. It seems to me that the sound was loud enough to be heard by everyone in the square behind us. Nothing. I rapped again even louder and more insistent.

All of a sudden there was a scraping noise and the little "talking window" peep hole in the door opened.

"What do you want? We're closed." An aggrieved voice asked in Greek. I don't speak Greek but that was obviously what was said.

Father Dmitri, our translator priest, instantly answered. There was quite a bit of conversation back and forth including some from the Varangian. All of a sudden we were startled as a little door built into the big door opened to let us in.

I had my shield and sword ready to use as I led the men into the barely lighted building. We rushed through the door ready to fight "because we'd been sent by the Patriarch to save the priests from the crusaders who were coming to kill them even if they don't want to be saved." *That was the best story we could think when we were back at our concession and we're sticking to it.*

Our sudden rush through the doorway scared the hell out of the priest who stood there holding a candle lantern. But he'd heard the explanation and soon recovered. Within seconds I'd left a man behind to guard the door and we were walking down the corridor towards the icon room with the door answerer's candle lantern lighting the way.

The door answerer was an Orthodox priest and he chattered away with our translator and the Varangian as we moved along the corridor. I walked behind them and wished I could see where we were going and understood what they were saying.

After walking down the corridor for what seemed like quite a while, we turned a corner and could see the flickering light of many candles and hear the murmur of prayers and subdued voices.

******

The priests surrounding the icons and praying looked up as we entered, but they kept on with their chanting and praying. Their prayers partially died away as the priest who answered the door went from one prayerful priest to the next and whispered in his ear.

Some of the priests looked relieved at what they were hearing and began to stand up; about a third of them, five or six, looked aggrieved at being interrupted and tried to wave the door answerer away. *Hot damn and yes, yes, yes; the icons are still here.*

"Out the door. Hurry. Follow that man." I finally began shouting at the slowly departing priests as I waved my sword towards the door and the archer standing next to it wearing the strange pointed hat that identified him as one of the emperor's guards. My translator and the Varangian began shouting and gesturing as well.

Most of the priests and monks headed for the door. Some did not. *And where the hell is Captain William and the column? They should have been here long ago.*

My translator began speaking loudly to those who refused to go—and then, after a few moments, he began shouting at them also.

"You must hurry. The Patriarch wants you safely away from here before the crusaders and Venetians arrive. It is an order from the Patriarch and you must be obedient and obey it. The Varangians are here to guard the icons."

"It's a sin that I lied but that's what I told them" my translator confided to me in a low voice after he said it. "But some didn't want to go."

As soon as the priests willing to leave had all hurried out of the room I took my sword and advanced on the others who were still sitting on the floor and praying. I pinked one of them in the thigh and he yelped in surprise and then he really screamed and stood up as I stabbed my sword at his arm and pinked him once again.

"Go as the Patriarch has ordered or die here and now for being disobedient to your vows."

That's what I had my translator priest tell them as I moved from man to man jabbing my sword at them. They scrambled to their feet with astonished looks on their faces.

My wide-eyed priest translator repeated my words to the priests in Greek as the shocked men began to scramble to their feet and stare at me in surprise. A few seconds later they began running for the door to get away from the madman who was bent on killing them.

"See them to the door and make sure they follow the others and leave as the Patriarch ordered. Take them to our camp unless they want to stay in the city." I snarled at one of the archers. He nodded and rushed out of the room behind them. *Now to business.*

"Quick," I shouted at my remaining men as I sheathed my sword and picked up a gold encrusted hand. "We need to move the icons to someplace safe until the captain and our men get here."

That's when I heard the faint shout of alarm in English from the archer I'd left at the front door.

******

I dropped some saint's gold covered hand back down into its golden box and rushed down the corridor to the open front door—and stared in horror at what I saw in the little square. The first light of dawn had arrived and crusaders were pouring into the square.

The crowd that had been in the square had disappeared and I could see the priests we just pushed out the door running for their lives and disappearing into the distant lane we had travelled to get here. Hopefully they're following the archer who had been told to lead them back to our camp outside the city wall.

I pointed down the corridor and shouted "bar the door

and run down that way to make sure the other entrances are barred. Hurry"

That's what I shouted at the archers as I stepped back into corridor and began running down the corridor in the other direction to make sure the other doors into the building are barred. There must be more doors and I don't even know where they are. *William and the men better get here soon.*

There was a door to the outside at the end of the corridor. It was barred so I didn't even slow down—I turned right and kept going down the next corridor. Two of the archers were running right behind me. Ahead of me I could hear faint noise and voices and the sound of things breaking.

The noise got much louder as I turned the next corner and skidded to a halt as I saw who was making it—there was an open door and I could see three crusaders with drawn swords in the light coming through the open door. They were standing over the body of one of the priests who had initially refused to stop praying. *Men-at-arms, my mind registered; not knights wearing armour.*

The three crusaders all turned and looked as I came around the corner. We'd surprised each other. One of them started to say something and turned towards me as my training kicked in. I dropped my shield and sword and pulled my bow off my shoulder and an arrow from my quiver in one fast motion. It's one of the moves Henry makes the archers practise every day both on land and when they are at sea, except on Sundays, of course.

The nearest crusader was still turning towards me and

shouting a warning when I grunted and pushed out my first arrow.

He was only twenty paces away—it was an easy shot and I pushed it out with everything I had. It went into him almost all the way to the fletching feathers. As he staggered backwards and sideways from the hit I could see half the arrow and its point sticking out of his back and a look of surprise and amazement on his face.

A split second later I pushed an arrow at a second man who started to leap over my kill to get to me with his sword. He twisted as he moved to avoid the first crusader and I hit him in the side. Right after my arrow struck two others went straight into his chest about six inches apart— the two archers behind me had arrived and at this range we could not miss.

The crusader began screaming a high pitched scream as he went over backwards from the force of the three strikes. His screams continued even whilst we each put an arrow into the third crusader as he turned and tried to get out of the door—and then the high pitched screams of dying crusader faded away as his legs began trembling and he finished his dying. It was all over in seconds.

I dropped my bow, swept up my sword, and rushed to shut and bar the door. As I did I could see a handful of crusaders walking cautiously down the little alley behind the door. They'd obviously seen the open door and heard the screams and were coming to investigate.

For some reason whilst I was lifting the heavy wooden bar into place a thought flashed into my mind that it was a good thing I decided to wear my chain—even though I always wear it. It's funny what you think of right after a fight, isn't it?

Chapter Seventeen
William

It was dark and we were lost. Somehow we have gone past the lane where we should have turned left to walk to the Patriarch's residence. We know we've come too far because in the moonlight and the very first light of dawn we can see vague the outline of big gate towers on either side of the next city gate.

The Varangian confirmed it through our interpreter.

"We've come too far, Captain. Those are the guard towers of the market gate up ahead. We must have missed the lane going up to the Patriarch's residence when the clouds covered the moon."

"Halt the column." *Goddamn it all to hell.* "Pass the word that we've missed the turn and that we'll be going back the other way at the double to find it."

After I gave the order I led my interpreter priest and the Varangian back through the long line of archers who'd been following us three abreast to join Henry at the rear of the column— which will now become its head as we hurry back the other way.

******

When we reached Henry at what had been the rear of

the column he took one glance at the look on my face and never said a word. Just shook his head sadly and nodded his agreement. Then I nodded and he gave the order to "double time" and we began retracing our steps as fast as possible.

We found the lane and turned into it. *How we missed it I'll never know; hopefully we found it in time.*

People scattered out of our way and stepped into doorways as we came down the lane at the double with our drums beating the step and still three abreast. After a while Henry shouted an order and the drums stopped so that every man could run at his own pace and we wouldn't be announcing our presence.

******

It was almost half an hour after sunrise when Henry and I and the two hundred and fifty archers double timing along behind us turned the corner and burst into the cobblestoned square in front of the Patriarch's residence.

We'd arrived not a moment too soon—the square was filled with crusaders milling about and a group of them were clustered around the entrance to the Patriarch's residence trying to batter in the door. Other crusaders were coming and going through the double doors of the church at the end of the square. The sun had not even fully come up.

This is not good but it's better than nothing—Peter and our men are obviously in the residence and the crusaders are attacking them which means we won't be breaking our contract if we attempt to defend them.

"Form a fighting line on the captain and pick off your targets." ... "Form a fighting line on the captain and pick off your targets." Henry shouted the order in his great loud voice. The sergeants behind us picked up Henry's order and repeated it as we swarmed into the square.

I had not led the archers very far into the square when our arrows, including mine, began flying and the crusaders began running—some towards us waving their swords, others ran the other way. Initially, most of them just gawked in astonishment as the first of our storm of arrows fell on them. Then they dropped whatever they were carrying and ran every which way in great confusion. *There is nothing like discovering someone is trying to kill you to unbalance one's thinking.*

"You need to move forward, Captain; there isn't enough room behind us for all of the men to get into the square." Henry said it to me with a grunt as he stood next to me and pushed an arrow out towards one of the rapidly dwindling number of crusaders running towards us and an almost certain death.

"Damn, you're right. Thank you, Lieutenant, for reminding me." I replied with my own grunt as I pushed one of mine at the only man still standing at the door to the Patriarch's residence and began walking forward. All the other crusaders who'd been at the door were already down or fleeing. *I'd started moving forward and looking at men in the square as soon as I pushed it out so I never did find out if my arrow flew true.*

In less than a minute there were a dozen or more dead crusaders in the square and we were the only ones alive in the square except for another dozen or so wounded crusaders abandoned by their friends. It's a good thing we caught the crusaders by surprise—the best thing you could say of our little skirmish is that the crusaders were even more surprised and disorganized and unready to fight than we were.

Henry held the men in line and tried to get them organized in case of a counter attack as I dashed towards the door of the Patriarch's Residence with my interpreter and my little squad of personal guards. Some of the other archers started to follow, good lads all and appreciated, but Henry called them back.

***** *Lieutenant Peter*

We'd barred the back door that opened into the alley just in time. One of the crusaders, the first one to go down, was having a bit of trouble dying. So I chopped him with my sword to help him on his way. As I did it dawned on me there might be yet another door somewhere.

"Quick Michael," I shouted to one of the archers. "Take Roger and keep going that way to see if there are any more doors that need barring. I'll go the other way around and meet you at the other end of the building."

Then we left the three crusaders in the corridor and ran like the devil was snapping at our heels.

I came past the barred front door and the men still waiting there at a dead run.

"Follow me," I shouted as I pounded past them. "They're all around us and there may be more doors." *Goddamn it; where the hell are William and Henry?*

There was another door to the side of the icon room at the end of the building. It was double barred and looked as though it hadn't been opened in years. Michael and Roger had already reached it and I was breathing hard by the time the rest of the men and I got there.

"We're in good shape. All the doors are barred. Now all we have to do is keep them out for a little whilst until the rest of our men get here." *I most sincerely hope.*

I assigned two men to each door and named one of them at each door to run to fetch us if anyone tried to break in. Then I walked back to the front door to catch my breath and see what I could see.

What I could see through the peep hole in the big front door was a cobblestone square full of crusaders milling about and using their hands to drink water from the horse trough in front of the church—and then I jumped in surprise as suddenly there was an eye trying to look in the peep hole not six inches from mine trying to look out. He must have been standing to one side and, from the way he jumped back; he was as surprised to see me as I was to see him.

"Open the door." I heard in French as someone pushed on the door to see if it would open. Then there were hard loud knocks. Someone was using his sword handle to pound on the wood.

At first I did not answer. But then the shouting and knocking continued and got more demanding so I shouted through the peep hole without opening the door.

"Go away and do your duty. The gold is buried in the church basement. This building has been taken for Lord

Boniface." *Maybe that will buy us some time.*

"What's that? What did you say about the gold?" A voice asked in Norman French from the other side of the door.

"The priests we just tortured said the missing gold is buried in the dungeon of the church," I answered.

******

There was some shouting in front of the door and through the peep hole I could see a couple of the crusaders begin running towards the entrance to the church. At least I think that's where they and everyone else was going when the two men immediately in front of the peep hole moved to one side and passed out of my sight.

A few minutes later and I discovered how wrong I was. Suddenly there was more shouting and banging on the door.

"Open the door or we'll knock it down."

This time when I looked out I could see a dozen or so determined looking crusaders—and two of them were carrying a heavy beam that they obviously intended to use as a battering ram. *Oh damn.*

"Wait. Wait. Don't do anything stupid. I'll go get his lordship and ask him if it's agreeable to let you in."

Then I turned to the two archers who were at the door with me and the Varangian and the priest translator and urgently in a low voice told them to run and fetch all the men at the other doors.

A few moments later there was more loud hails from outside the door. First in a language I didn't understand, probably Italian, from one of the men in front of the peep hole. But then he stepped to the side so I couldn't see him and another took his place, a big fellow with great huge beard. He was obviously a knight and he spoke French. Worse, he wasn't a knight in shining armour, his armour was battered and his tunic was ripped. He was a fighting man for sure. *If we fight we've got to kill this one early on.*

"Are you going to open the door or not?" He called out in French.

"Wait damn you. Just wait a minute," I answered. "Sir Edmund's gone to fetch him. ... He's found a woman if you must know and he's got her somewhere. Or maybe he's still questioning the priests. This is a big place you know". .. and then after a pause I added "and he's going to be angry for you interfering so you better go get your lord to talk to him." *All I could do was play for time.*

"Oh Damn!" I exclaimed again as my men ran up. They didn't believe my story—through the peep hole I could see the men outside getting ready to use the ram.

"Bows," I hissed to my men standing behind me as I turned away from the door. "Follow me. Use your heavies. One of the bastards is wearing armour."

I moved about thirty paces away from the door and arrayed my men across the corridor. And, of course, the corridor was only wide enough for five of us to stand side by side with enough room to shoot. So I sent other three men further down to guard our rear where the corridor turns towards the icon room. *Anyone dashing around the corner to join the fight is going to suddenly find themselves at close-quarters with my rear guard and get a big surprise; that Varangian's axe looks vicious.*

The Varangian seemed particularly pleased to be sent to the rear. He gripped his shield and axe tightly and gave me a tight grin and a determined nod when I arrayed the archers across the corridor and sent him and one archer and the translator priest further back. Until that moment he probably wasn't sure that he was really one of us such that we wouldn't sacrifice him by putting him into the most dangerous position.

We were as ready as we could be when the crusaders with the big wooden timber began to use it to batter in the door. It only took three big hits before they knocked the heavy wooden door off the wall and into the corridor where we waited. Crusaders immediately pushed their way in over the fallen door waving their swords—and began to die.

The distance between the attacking crusaders and us was close enough for an experienced archer to shoot with great accuracy. And we were all very experienced archers. The first four men who lurched into the corridor in one big mass went down quickly, almost every one with multiple arrows including the veteran knight with five or six. I saw the shock and surprise in his eyes when he was first hit and realised his armour wasn't going to protect him.

At least two of the crusaders and maybe three were able to back out in time to live, temporarily in the case of one with an arrow deep in his side. Two of the four down in the corridor were still alive. One was screaming.

"Don't waste your arrows; let them die by themselves." I said as I crept slowly down the corridor to see what I could see through the door opening.

What I saw caused me to give a great whoop of joy and shout "Yes! Yes!" as I pumped my arm up and down. There were dead and wounded men in front of the door and chaos and confusion in the square as a great storm of arrows rained down. One fool actually tried to run in through the open doorway to get to safety. He got all the way in and fell with at least half a dozen arrows sticking in him including two of mine.

I cut the throats of the two crusaders on the floor who were still alive whilst we waited for our men to arrive.

Chapter Eighteen
William

Peter was standing in the doorway to the Patriarch's residence as my little squad of guards and my translator and I came puffing up. There were screams and shouts in the square behind me as Henry's men finished off the wounded crusaders and began collecting the crusaders' swords and armour and picking up the arrows and arrowheads that could be salvaged.

"We missed the turn. Are you alright?" I asked Peter.

"I figured as much," Peter answered. "It was a close call as you can see but we all made it—and we've got the relics. The priests are gone."

"Yes, I know," I said. "We met some of them as we

came down the lane. We'll talk later. Right we've got to get the relics on the wagons. We've got to get out of here before the crusaders regroup and come back."

And that's exactly what we did.

******

We loaded the relics on Harold's galley and Tori and I sailed for Cornwall two days later via Cyprus and Malta. Before I left I sent a parchment to Boniface telling him that a force of his men attacked a squad of my archers guarding the Patriarch's residence and that one of my men was wounded—and that if it ever happens again I will consider our agreement ended and he's going to lose a lot more than the couple of dozen of his crusaders who went down in front of my archers.

Our only casualty on the raid turned out to be Roger, the son of the miller's apprentice from Crawley. We found his body as we were returning to our concession with the relics.

-End of the Book -

I sincerely hope you enjoyed reading *The Missing Treasure* as much as I enjoyed writing it. If so, I would respectfully request a brief review on Amazon and elsewhere with five stars so as to encourage others to read it as well. I can be reached at martinarcherV@gmail.com and would enjoy, and greatly value, hearing your opinion of the book.

Please read more. The rest of the action-packed books in this great saga of medieval England are all available on Kindle as eBooks and some are available in print. You can find them by going to your Amazon website and searching for *Martin Archer fiction*. A collection of the first six books is available on Kindle as *The Archers' Story*. Similarly, a collection of the next four novels in the saga is available as *The Archers' Story: Part II,* and there are additional books in the saga beyond those four.

Amazon eBooks in the exciting and action-packed *The Company of Archers* saga:

The Archers
The Archers' Castle
The Archer's War
The Archer's Return
Rescuing the Hostages
Kings and Crusaders
The Archers' Gold
The Missing Treasure
Castling the King
The Sea Warriors
The Captain's Men
Gulling the Kings
The Archers' Magna Carta

Amazon eBooks in Martin Archer's exciting and action-packed *Soldier and Marines* saga:

Soldier and Marines
Peace and Conflict

War Breaks Out
War in the East
Israel's Next War

Collections
The Archer's Story - books I, II, III, IV, V, VI
The Archer's Story II - books VII, VIII, IX, X,
Soldiers and Marines Trilogy

Other eBooks you might enjoy:
Cage's Crew by Martin Archer writing as Raymond Casey
America's Next War by Michael Cameron

Made in the USA
Middletown, DE
14 August 2018